Everything was as usual that summer evening in Little
Mowlesbury – mothers preparing meals, children playing cricket on the green, spoilt little Ashley on his way
to bed – except for one thing: a brilliant star that
appeared, came nearer and nearer, and finally, with a
tearing shriek of blasting jets mixed with a thunder that
stopped your heart beating, landed on the cricket pitch,
burning the grass to a fine, grey powder.

It was a space craft – a secret one – and before anyone
could protest the man inside had kidnapped the first
children who came flocking to see it, and lifted the ship
far into the sky again. And then they discovered that he
was dying and they had to find out how to work the
ship.

'Me tell you?' he gasped. 'Me tell you how the thing
works? Look, I got radiation burns that will kill me in
a week learning what I learned and I don't know
anything!'

This book is both a first-class science-fiction story and
an interesting study of conflict between two boys –
Brylo, the weak boy with brains, and Tony, the bully
who had courage – each of whom felt he should take the
decisions which would help the children out of their
dreadful danger. Also in Puffins: *Trillions*, *Grinny*, *Time
Trap*, *Antigrav*, *A Rag, a Bone and a Hank of Hair*, *Wheelie
in the Stars*, *On the Flip Side*, *Robot Revolt* and *Sweets from
a Stranger*.

For readers of ten and over.

Nicholas Fisk

Space Hostages

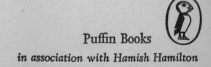

Puffin Books
in association with Hamish Hamilton

Puffin Books, Penguin Books Ltd, Harmondsworth, Middlesex, England
Viking Penguin Inc., 40 West 23rd Street, New York, New York 10010, U.S.A.
Penguin Books Australia Ltd, Ringwood, Victoria, Australia
Penguin Books Canada Ltd, 2801 John Street, Markham, Ontario, Canada L3R 1B4
Penguin Books (N.Z.) Ltd, 182–190 Wairau Road, Auckland 10, New Zealand

First published by Hamish Hamilton 1967
Published in Puffin Books 1970
Reprinted 1971, 1972, 1976 (twice), 1978, 1980, 1982, 1983, 1985

Made and printed in Great Britain by
Hazell Watson & Viney Limited,
Member of the BPCC Group,
Aylesbury, Bucks
Set in Linotype Juliana

Chapter 1

Billy Bason intended to send down an offbreak. It turned into a yorker as a single, spiteful ray from the setting sun shone through the trees right into his eye. Tony Hoskings made his usual flashy swipe at the ball and as usual connected. The ball hissed away into the long grass, already dew-drenched, looking for somewhere to hide.

Tony Hoskings yelled, 'Come ON then ! RUN !'

He pelted up and down between the wickets – sticks draped with coats – with his single pad flapping and leaking its stuffing and his blond mop jigging and his bony legs and arms pumping. He looked like a puppet gone mad.

'Bung it IN !' yelled Spadger Garrett, at the wicket.

'Can't find it !' shouted Tiddler from the edge of the meadow. 'LOST BALL !' the other fielders chorused maliciously, not bothering to join the search.

'What do you mean, lost ball? That's my twentieth run, lost ball or no. I got my twenty !' Tony Hoskings swore, knocked down a wicket and kicked the coats. No one took much notice. They were playing so late because they had to, not because they wanted to. If Tony did not get what he wanted, there would be trouble.

'It's all right, Tony, you got your twenty,' said Sandra Rumsey. And then – forgetting all about cricket and fielding and keeping Tony Hoskings in a good temper – she pointed to the deepening blue of the evening sky.

'Look at that !' she said. 'I've never seen a star that big !'

'That's the evening star,' someone said.

'It's Polaris,' said Brylo Deniz confidently. He was so sure that he did not bother to look. Brylo was generally right about such things.

This time he was completely wrong.

'Oh no you don't, missy!' said Beauty's mother, Mrs Hopcroft.

'Get off your Dad and up to bed this instant. And you drink your milk, mind!' Her father pulled her hair and said, 'Torment!'

Beauty climbed down off her father's lap. She cupped her pink-white hands round the blue mug of milk and Mrs Hopcroft thought of cyclamens and periwinkles. Beauty shook back her hair and her mother thought of a glass of honey standing in the sun. Beauty smiled and her mother found herself beaming fatuously.

This was not just a mother's doting pride. Beauty's teeth were white and tiny and perfect. Beauty's feet under her nightie were as pretty as sugar mice. It was not her parents that had first called her 'Beauty' instead of her real name, Maureen; perhaps it had been old Mrs Durden, who kept the shop where Beauty spent her Saturday threepence; or Jim Knowles, the landlord of the Ploughshare, who bribed smiles from her with lemonade; or anyone else in Little Mowlesbury barring the Vicar, who called her 'Little One' (he could not remember names) and Tony Hoskings, who called her 'Blondie' or 'Tich'.

Beauty kissed her mother and father and went up the narrow stairs to her bedroom, counting each stair aloud. This was her ritual each night. But tonight, it was broken. Beauty stopped by the little window halfway up the staircase.

'Oh, Mummy, come and look!' she cried. 'There's a big star in the sky!'

Beauty was wrong. It was not a star.

The boy and girl cricketers straggled back from the meadow with bats and pads and stumps. They pushed and hollered round Tony Hoskings, easily the tallest and most powerful of them – half a head taller than Brylo Deniz, though he too was eleven years old.

'I told you I'd get that twenty!' said Tony. 'I got my twenty before you lost the ball!' No one argued. Without interrupting himself, he left the road, squelched into the edge of the foul pond where ducks had once swum and marched over the roof of the half-submerged carcase of an Austin Heavy 12. 'Well, come ON, then! Follow yer leader! That's me!' he yelled, and all the others followed him. Squelch, squelch, thump, scrabble, DOING, DOING, pause, jump, splash, squelch, squelch. The line of figures rose and fell like a caterpillar climbing over a twig. Brylo Deniz hesitated, shrugged and followed the rest. But even then, Tony went for him.

'Heh! Where's Brylo gone, then?' shouted Tony. 'Anyone here seen Brylo?' Some of the boys sniggered. It was best to laugh at Tony's jokes. And this was one of them.

'Oh! Sorry, Brylo boy! Didn't see you!' said Tony. 'Couldn't see you in this light. I mean, how could I?'

More uneasy laughter. For Brylo's skin was dark brown. He was a Jamaican or West Indian or something like that; an orphan adopted by a childless couple in the village. Brylo was clever at school – two forms ahead of Tony. And Tony was leader –

'That's never a star!' piped the Tiddler, eight-year-old Brian Biddle. They all paused and stared at the brilliant dot in the sky. 'There's never been a star that big!'

And it was not a star...

'I'm off!' muttered Spadger to Brylo. They had reached his cottage and Spadger could see through the heavy dropping lace curtains that the telly was on. If only Tony didn't see him go....

'I want you, Spadger!' yelled Tony. He had not even bothered to turn his head, thought Spadger, he just knew

I'd try and slide off home. 'All of you!' Tony bellowed. 'We're going to serenade Dirty Durdens.'

'Why can't you leave them alone, they haven't done you any harm,' began Sandra. But Tony just turned on his heel and looked at her, his eyes glinting in the dusky light.

'You *sing*, see?' he said, hoarsely.

They were at the shop now. You could just read the familiar, ancient signs that covered its front. TIZER THE APPETIZER. NOSEGAY. BIRD'S EYE. And Sandra could see in her mind's eye the musty, gaslit back parlour, with old Mr Durden mumbling and dozing in his stiff wooden chair and old Mrs Durden blinking and shuffling and dratting the cat. Sandra was once a Brownie, she had been inside there to clean. It was dark and sad. The rest sounded feeble but Tony's voice was hoarse and piercing as a carrion crow's:

DIRTY OL' DURDEN
GIVES SHORT WEIGHT
EATS DEAD TOM CATS
OFF A DIRTY PLATE

And sure enough, the backdoor was flung open and old Mr Durden came out as if he'd been thrown out, and he was raving and mumbling and prancing and Tony was braying with laughter and dancing round him, just out of reach.

All the children ran. Not because they were frightened but because they were embarrassed. Even Tony soon gave up and came scarecrowing down the dim road after them.

Behind them, old Mrs Durden scolded old Mr Durden and told him not to fret – come inside and eat your supper *do*. And because he was so old, he forgot the children and stared about him with his watery eyes.

'Never seen a star the like of that!' he said. And so brilliant was the light of the thing that looked like a star that it made his eyes blink even faster.

The group began to break up, bit by bit, as the children reached their homes.

''Night, Tiddler, mind it when you wash – you might slip down the plug'ole !'

'Come inside this instant, Sandra, your supper's spoiling.'

Inside most of the houses and cottages, the telly was on and the places were laid.

'Do switch off the telly, Dad, it makes me sick, the news !'

'Hold on a minute, Mother, I want to hear it . . .'

'Sit up straight and eat your good food properly, my lad . . .'

'It's always the same these days – *they'll* drop a bomb or we'll drop a bomb !'

'Let's hear it, then.'

The man on the telly made it all sound very normal and respectable. 'Mr Tang replied that unless effective guarantees for the unmolested independence of Pian Tuk were offered immediately by the Western Powers, he would have no option but to use nuclear weapons. In the Commons today, the Prime Minister said that Mr Tang's threats were hardly likely to influence the course of action decided upon by Her Majesty's government and supported by the whole free world. We too had nuclear weapons and would not hesitate to –'

'Oh, must we listen to this, it makes me –'

'No, keep quiet a minute –'

'. . . In America, attitudes towards the Pian Tuk situation are hardening. The Defence Secretary, Mr O'Rourke, said today that America wants peace and will fight for it if necessary. Promises had been made and broken. The American nation would not tolerate –'

'Hold your fork properly, do !'

'Threats and bombs and fighting. Haven't we had enough ? It makes me sick, I don't know why you listen to it –'

'And now,' said the man on the telly, with a quick smirk, 'cricket !'

'Mum, we saw a whopping great star when we were playing cricket, big as a saucer !'

'Eat up. Your pudding's ready.'

Ashley Mott did not play cricket. He was afraid of Tony Hoskings – and besides, there was his mother. Mother did not like the village boys and girls, they were rude and rough. Mother and Daddy (but especially Mother) were ... *nicer* than the village people. Mother had once known a little boy who had been hit by a cricket ball and they had to take his eye out. His eye OUT!

Earlier, Ashley had heard them playing cricket on the meadow.

'Howzat!' lots of voices shouted. 'OUT!' shouted the umpire. Ashley had shivered then and he shivered now. His eye OUT!

He did not want to play cricket, thank you very much. Mother was right.

He continued undressing, for shortly his mother would call up the stairs, 'Ashley, ready for drinkies?' and he would say 'Yes, Mother! Nearly ready!' and she would say, 'Pop into your 'jamas and Mother will be up!' and she would bring him his warm Ovaltine in the bunny rabbit mug.

A cold, dew-laden draught of air stirred the curtains and Ashley went to close the window. The sky was dark blue overhead, but still pale where the sun had set. He reached forward for the window catch – and there, just behind the peak of the roof, was an enormous star!

'Mummy, Mummy!' he cried, 'Mummy, come and see! A huge star!'

Everyone was home now, but still there was talk of Little Mowlesbury's star.

'Heh! Look at the star! It's got bigger, Dad!' said Tony.

'I'll give you stars ...' said his father.

Spadger saw it. 'It can't be a star!' he said to himself.

Brylo saw it. 'It's moved, so it can't be a star,' he reasoned.

The telly was too dull to watch that night with all the

news flashes upsetting the proper programmes. So perhaps half a dozen children in Little Mowlesbury were staring at the 'star' when it went out. It went out like a light. One minute it was there and the next second it was gone.

And now that their eyes were not concentrated on the disc of light, their ears could hear a noise. No, not the transformers of the power substation – they made a lower, steadier hum. This noise was breathier, more whining, more urgent.

'Spaceship!' breathed Spadger to himself. 'I'll bet that's what it is! From Mars!'

'It must have been catching the last rays of the sun,' thought Brylo, 'and then the sun went down – or the star thing came lower and nearer – so it "went out". A spaceship?'

'Poor Mother's quite puffed out!' said Mrs Mott to Ashley.

'What a naughty boy you are! Big star, indeed!'

'But . . .' said Ashley.

'Give Mother a big kiss and straight off to Dreamland!' said Mrs Mott.

There was the noise of an express train, then twenty express trains – then a tearing shriek of blasting jets mixed with a thunder that shook glass and shifted tiles and stopped your heart beating – and IT landed in the middle of the meadow, burning the grass of the cricket pitch to fine grey powder.

Chapter 2

They poured out of the pub, the church, the British Legion hall, the parish hall and their houses and down to the meadow; the whole village, all 170 souls, even old Mr Durden.

They stopped at the edge of the meadow. They had not known what to expect. The reality was beyond imagination.

It was a vast craft. It would have covered twenty, thirty cricket pitches. It could have sheltered half a dozen great airliners. It was domed on top, slightly concave below (Spadger found himself comparing it to a monstrous hubcap from a car). It was as high off the ground as a house, or two double-decker buses standing on top of each other. It had four gleaming legs like a modern coffee table, with the same disc-like feet. Even in the almost faded light, it gleamed like porcelain containing metal particles.

It was completely silent and showed no lights. But sometimes a tuft of long grass flared briefly for a moment – the smell of burning grass was everywhere – and you could see a glinting reflection magnified in the shining belly of the ship.

People talked as they watched, but their voices were hushed as voices are in church when the service is about to start. A mild breeze blew more grass smoke towards them and some of them coughed. They waited.

They did not have to wait long. A trap in the belly of the craft opened with a slight whine and rumble and a metallic cabin whose floor was the size of the trap descended on a metal shaft. The noise of the descent was exactly that of a lift.

The descent took about ten seconds. The cabin reached the

scorched ground, appeared to sense its presence and stopped. So did the noise.

Suddenly, the whole area covered by the ship and the villagers was flooded with light! The shock drove the villagers back a pace. Someone said, 'Heaven preserve us!' and someone else said, 'Mind my feet!' Then several people said, 'Shush!' It seemed somehow dangerous even to whisper.

But then there was a slight jostling and Mr Gordon, the farmer, and Eric and Fred, his farmhands, were pushing their way to the front. All three had guns. Then, after more shuffling and murmurs of 'Mind out, now!' Jim Knowles joined Mr Gordon. Mr Knowles carried a service rifle. You could hear them muttering to each other.

'You cover it, but leave the accurate stuff to me, you've only got spreadshot in that ...'

'Aye, that's right, you pick 'un off, we'll cover ...'

'But leave it till you're sure, you know what I mean ...'

'Aye, the whites of their eyes.'

'Their tentacles more like!' brayed Fred, and some people laughed.

But only for a short while.

A minute went by and nothing happened.

Then came the Voice: an enormous voice that flooded the meadow and echoed off the belly of the ship.

'YOU WON'T NEED THOSE GUNS!' it roared. Then, 'OH, BLAST!' Then, much more quietly – 'Sorry, didn't mean to deafen you. Look, you won't need the guns, so for heaven's sake put them down. That's better. Now keep quite calm and leave the guns alone. I'm coming out. Right?'

The door of the cabin silently opened. And into the glare of the lights stepped an RAF Flight Lieutenant in his peaked cap and tunic with two rings. He touched a tiny microphone at his throat and said, 'Sorry if I startled you.' Then, 'Gosh, this ground is hot.'

Chapter 3

He was a very ordinary Flight Lieutenant, they discovered; a startling contrast to the ship he flew. They bombarded him with questions. It was surprising how few answers he had. Or was he just handling them very cleverly?

'These flying saucer things,' said Mr Knowles. 'How come we've never even been told about them – never even guessed they existed?'

'Oh, security, old man!' said the Flight Lieutenant.

'But what about all those stories in the papers – you know, unidentified flying objects, all that? Is this one of them?'

'Oh well, you know the newspapers, old man.'

'Well, how many of these things are there? Lots? Just this one?'

'Well, the powers that be don't exactly confide in me, you know. But I think this is the only one.'

'But what's it *for*? What does it *do*?'

'Oh, you could call it a multi-purpose craft. Definitely.'

Mr Knowles gave up. Spadger took over.

'Go on, tell us, mister. What'll she do?'

'You mean how fast will she go?'

'Yes, what'll she *do*?'

'Well over the speed of sound.'

'But lots of ordinary planes do that.'

'So they do. Yes,' said the Flight Lieutenant. Then he added, very vaguely, 'Good show!'

'Now this really won't do, young man!' said the Vicar. 'I'm going to ask you three questions and I want the an-

swers straight from the shoulder, man to man. Question One
– why did you land here? Question Two – when will you take
off again and leave us in peace? Question Three – who is your
chief or superior officer or whatever you call it?'

'Well, let's see, Padre. Why did I land here? Because I jolly
well had to. Question two, when will I take off again? – I
jolly well can't.'

'You can't?'

'Spot of bother. Had to come down. Question three – never
mind, Padre. Call it the R A F and leave it at that. O K?'

'Most certainly not! I'm going to telephone the Ministry
of Defence immediately. And the police.'

'No, Padre. Please don't!' The young Flight Lieutenant
seemed to pull himself together and become firmer and harder.
'Don't do that. I'll tell you why. I'll tell you all why.' He
touched the button on the throat microphone and his voice
could be heard by everyone. 'Listen! No telephoning or anything of that sort! I hope no one's telephoned already?'

'They couldn't do that without me!' said Miss Miggs. She
was the postmistress. 'I was in such a state when this thing
came down out of the sky, I simply flew here, and all the
lines...'

'Good. No telephoning, then. Now I'll tell you why. Have
you been following the news? The trouble in Pian Tuk and
so on?'

There was a low chorus of 'Aaah!' from the villagers.

'Then you can guess what I'm going to say. This craft is
secret. That's putting it mildly. It's a British secret – but more
than that. You could say that it's part of world affairs. A
very important part at this moment. So it's no good telephoning the Ministry of Defence. It's no good ringing up
the Income Tax people, even ...' (there was some laughter)
'... because what is happening here is bigger than all of
them put together. And I'll tell you this: THERE ARE
PLENTY OF PEOPLE THROUGHOUT THE WORLD WHO
WANT TO KNOW ABOUT THIS CRAFT! Not only where it

is, but if it EXISTS, even! And not all those people are friends of ours. Understood?'

'But surely someone ought to be told? The Government –?'

'The Vicar here says that someone ought to be told,' said the Flight Lieutenant's amplified voice. 'Well, Padre, so they should. But not, I repeat not, by telephone. Surely you've heard of telephones being tapped, listened in to? And surely you can guess what's already happened? No? Well, I'll tell you!' He paused and lit a cigarette. 'Look at this craft!' He flung out an arm and the villagers' heads turned to stare at the vast saucer, black now against the sky. 'Do you honestly think it's got a telephone exchange inside? Dial 999 and ask for Mars? No such luck! No nice cosy postmistress for us!'

There was a general laugh and heads turned to Miss Miggs.

'No, we don't do things quite that way. Our communications are to do with satellites in space and scrambled codes and security piled on security piled on security! Now, I can make the ship sit up and beg, even from here – look, I'll show you!'

They watched: and although the Flight Lieutenant seemed to touch nothing, they saw the cabin door open and close, a series of aerials emerge from the belly of the craft and then retract and – as a sort of encore – a single beam of light shoot from a hidden source on to the ground, along which it crawled until it 'found' and spotlit the Flight Lieutenant.

'Down, Fido!' said the Flight Lieutenant and the light went out. 'No, seriously,' continued the Flight Lieutenant, 'I can do a whole lot of things with this ship. But one of the things I can't do is break its communications, its codes, its links with higher authority. That's all built in and pro-grammed and going like mad. Surely you realize that even before I touched down here, the ship had told the whole story to the only people who ought to know!'

'Aaaah!' said the villagers again. They understood.

'Tell you what I'll do!' said the Flight Lieutenant. 'I'll let you hear it talking to our masters! Come on lad ...' he pulled Ashley, the nearest boy, forward. 'You can press the button and we'll all listen in! Go on, press it!'

He held out what looked like a particularly small transistor radio and indicated the right button. Ashley pressed it. The Flight Lieutenant put the little set to his throat microphone, and they heard a fluttering, whining chatter of electronic sounds – a gibberish that could have come from outer space.

'Well, that's the ship talking!' said the Flight Lieutenant, switching the noise off. 'And if anyone can translate, please let me know. I hope she's saying what I want to hear . . .'

'What's that, Flight Lieutenant?'

'Where I can get another packet of cigarettes. I'm out!' He flung an empty packet away and everyone laughed. Farmer Gordon was the first to succeed in thrusting a pack of cigarettes into the Flight Lieutenant's hand, but several packs were offered. It seemed that their terrifying visitor from the sky was not so terrible after all.

Chapter 4

A quarter of an hour later, the villagers and the Flight Lieutenant were old friends. He had arranged the microphone so that everyone within several yards of him could be heard and he could be heard by everyone. It was almost cosy sitting there in the warm summer night. The whole of the village had not felt such unity since the end of World War II. That had been wonderful. But this was staggering. A flying saucer in Little Mowlesbury!

'No, I just can't answer that sort of question,' said the Flight Lieutenant. 'Please don't ask me too much about the ship. You'll get me shot if I answer!'

'That's right!' said Fred. 'Play fair by the Lieut!'

'Anyhow,' said the Flight Lieutenant, 'even if I gave you a complete answer to the sort of questions your shrewd Vicar has been popping at me, I don't think you would understand me. Even if I showed you over the ship, you wouldn't see a single thing you understood except the chairs and tables.'

'Oh, mister!' said the Tiddler. 'You'd never let us see inside?'

'Let's see! Let's see!' the children pleaded. 'Go on, mister! Just a quick look!'

'The Flight Lieutenant has already explained,' began the Vicar, but nothing would quieten the children. 'Do let's see!' they begged.

The Flight Lieutenant shook his head steadily against the torrent of voices. Smiling, he lifted his hand. The chorus died down. 'All you'd get by going aboard is a trip in that cabin-lift and ...' But he had said the wrong thing. Everyone wanted to go up in the lift. This time it was harder to silence the children.

'Sorry, kids!' said the Flight Lieutenant. 'That ship isn't mine. It's not my property.'

'Well, who *does* it belong to, then?' shouted the Tiddler and lots of people laughed.

'Taxpayer's property, sonny!' said the Flight Lieutenant, smiling.

'My dad's a taxpayer!' shouted the Tiddler.

'Aye, all our dads are taxpayers!' yelled the children. The laughter increased.

'Our young friends would rather seem to have established their claim,' the Vicar chuckled. The grown-ups chortled and nodded.

But the Flight Lieutenant suddenly changed the mood. 'What's the time? Half past? For heaven's sake! Give me that radio!' He snatched a transistor set from Tony's hand, tuned it rapidly and listened, his face set hard. It was the news.

'They've gone and done it!' he said, a few moments later. 'They've issued an ultimatum!' He switched the radio off and gave it back to Tony without looking at him. Everyone was silent. The Flight Lieutenant stared straight ahead of himself. The silence lengthened.

'Taxpayers' money! TAXPAYERS' MONEY!' he suddenly shouted.

'My Lord, you're right! You and me – we've all paid our money! Now we take our choice! You want to see inside the craft, sonny?'

'Yes! Yes!' said Tiddler.

'Yes!' cried the others.

'Well, you might as well get some pleasure for all the money you paid!' said the Flight Lieutenant viciously. 'All right, then! All right! All aboard the Skylark! Taxpayers' money! Come on, then! Children first, six at a time! Then the rest of you! All aboard the Skylark!'

Beauty, of course, found her royal way to the front. The others pushed and jostled and shoved. Beauty carefully placed her little slippered foot on the step of the 'lift', and smiled a polite and pearly smile at the Flight Lieutenant and entered. Once inside, she turned and waved to her parents and said, 'Look at me! I'm in!'

'Oh, Beauty, come back!' cried her mother, suddenly afraid. But it was too late. 'AND the next please!' said the Flight Lieutenant, imitating a bus conductor.

Tiddler went next because he was small. His small body and big head, with its 'Mowlesbury Massacre' pudding basin haircut, were brilliantly lit as he went in. He blinked, smiled and blushed.

'AND a lady, IF you please!' said the Flight Lieutenant, still being a bus conductor.

Sandra Rumsey went in. She wore a fawn dressing-gown over her pyjamas and her very long, thick, brown plait swung as she bent down to take Beauty's hand. 'There's our Sandra,' said her mother wonderingly. And you knew what she meant. For Sandra's wide, friendly, homely face and her nice old dressing-gown looked strange in the little metallic room, with its slick brushed-aluminium walls.

Brylo went in, his face solemn and his eyes wide. This was the entry to the world he knew was to be his – the world of the brain, an international world where the colour of your skin meant very much less than the size of your cranium. His parents watched him without expression. They understood. They had reason to: for his parents-by-adoption were 'foreigners' in the village – Mr Deniz, a South American, was an assistant in a biological laboratory. He worked in a nest of concrete buildings some miles from Little Mowlesbury. He knew the villagers had a vague and on the whole kindly contempt for him and for Brylo. He felt just the same distant contempt for them. Nothing ever happened in Little Mowlesbury: but things, real things, happened in the laboratories. He and Brylo talked about these things ...

'Another lovely lady, then!' said the Flight Lieutenant, still jolly. But he looked strangely worn and ill in the light from the lift. A girl called Diana Moyce went forward, then back, then forward, and began to giggle and clutch her friends' arms.

'*Flip!*' said Tony Hoskings, and pushed past her into the lift. He stood there, a head taller than the others, throwing his lank yellow hair back impatiently and daring anyone to challenge him. No one did. He was in.

Diana went in. 'Come back, Di!' 'Go on, Di!' her friends shouted. There was so much screaming and excitement that she had to go in, really, she told herself. And Tony was there. Diana was tall and coltish like Tony. She was twelve and wished she were eighteen. She *felt* eighteen. She rolled her big, dark, bold eyes and smoothed her long black hair nervously and shouted to Tony, 'Hey, Tone! All these flipping kids . . .'

Spadger Garrett and Billy Bason went in together, before anyone could stop them. 'You come out of that, you young limb!' shouted Spadger's father, but Spadger pretended not to understand and shouted back, 'Yes, I'm all right, Dad!' The two boys stood there beaming awkwardly – Billy all freckles and sandiness, Spadger mousy and plump. They did most things together, including ferreting, catapulting, attempting to ride cows, brewing gunpowder that didn't explode and sloe gin that did.

'Better than the fair!' said Spadger.

'That's all for the first trip!' said the Flight Lieutenant.

'Really, these village children,' said Mrs Mott, eyeing Diana. Diana caught the look. 'Why, how simply divine, it's Mrs Mott!' she screeched, 'How-jerdo, my deah!'

Mrs Mott was so shocked by this attack that she let go Ashley's hand and put her own hands to her burning cheeks.

'That's all for the first trip!' said the amplified voice of the Flight Lieutenant.

Disturbed as she was, Mrs Mott saw how ill he looked.

That horrible girl Diana and this horrible spaceship and now this man, this Flight Lieutenant. All of a sudden, she felt sick with fright, she knew there was something amiss, something not nice . . .

'Ashley!' she cried. He had slipped away!

'Up we go, then!' said the Flight Lieutenant.

'What about me?'

'And me!'

'Back for another trip round the Skylark later – parents too!' said the Flight Lieutenant.

'Ashley!' screamed Mrs Mott. Her red nails clawed at the throat of her velvet dress. The whining noise of the lift door and the sliding door shifted, and began to slide shut.

And she saw Ashley, clean and pink and white and neat in his warm dressing-gown, slip as cunningly as a stoat through the closing gap and into the lift. She saw the door close. And she knew as certainly as she knew the neatly brushed and parted hair – she could just glimpse it as the door shut – that her Ashley was going to be involved in some sort of dreadful trouble.

'Back in half a minute for the next . . .' said the Flight Lieutenant from inside the lift. Then there was a metallic click as if he had disconnected some vital plug. Then the whirring whine as the lift ascended, a little glimmer of light rising up into the belly of the ship. Then the closing of the underbelly doors so that one could no longer see that there had been a lift at all. Then another click, and the voice of the Flight Lieutenant, speaking through a louder, harsher amplifier and in a louder, harsher tone:

'CLEAR THE GROUND. Get away from the ship. Clear the ground. GET WELL AWAY. CLEAR THE GROUND.'

Mrs Mott screamed first. There were more screams, then a roar of voices and a surging of the crowd under the ship. The four guns were raised, but the Flight Lieutenant's voice said, 'None of that!' and the guns wavered and were brought down.

'He must have TV in there,' began Jim Knowles.

'YOU HAVE TEN SECONDS,' said the great metal voice, flatly. 'NINE . . . EIGHT . . . SEVEN   YOU'D BETTER MOVE AND MOVE FAST! – SIX – CLEAR THE GROUND, FIVE . . .'

Some people moved and one or two ran.

'FOUR . . . THREE . . . TWO . . .' A whole crowd ran for the edge of the meadow.

'ONE! ALL RIGHT. I TOLD YOU TO MOVE . . .'

There was a thunderous bellow from the black shape above them – a sound so loud that people screamed from the pain of it and fell to the ground, their hands over their ears. The bellowing stopped. Slowly the figures rose and walked, dazed. The voice spoke again.

'YOU HAVE A MATTER OF SECONDS. HELP EACH OTHER OFF THE GROUND. CLEAR THE GROUND. I AM GOING TO TAKE OFF.'

The Vicar looked up at the glinting metallic blackness, and whispered, 'But you said you couldn't! You lied!' Next to him old Durden fell down and lay gasping.

'CLEAR THE GROUND. CLEAR THE GROUND. YOU PEOPLE THERE AROUND THE OLD MAN – LIFT HIM UP AND GET HIM AWAY. DO IT NOW. CLEAR THE GROUND. I AM GOING TO TAKE OFF.'

'Ashley!' screamed Mrs Mott. She ran to one of the great legs of the ship and hit it with her fists.

'CLEAR THE GROUND. GET THAT WOMAN AWAY. YOU TWO MEN, TAKE THAT WOMAN AWAY. CLEAR THE GROUND, YOU HAVE VERY LITTLE TIME.'

A new noise, a thin electronic scream, came from the ship. The scream rose higher and higher and settled to a single steady note. 'THAT'S RIGHT, CLEAR THE GROUND. THAT'S GOOD. NOW KEEP WALKING. WALK AWAY. GET WELL CLEAR. KEEP WALKING. GET WELL CLEAR. YOU HAVE ONLY SECONDS LEFT!'

Women were crying and stumbling. Knowles fired six shots from his rifle in quick succession. You could see the spark and glitter where the bullets hit the ship. The Flight Lieutenant's voice, suddenly quiet and tired, said, 'Don't be a silly man.' Then the voice came back, not so loud.

'Now, listen. Your children are coming with me. As long as I last. They will find a way, somewhere, somehow. Away from this world.' The voice faltered.

'He's ill,' whispered the Vicar.

'He's mad,' said Mr Knowles.

Almost as if he had heard him, the Flight Lieutenant said, 'Perhaps you think I am mad. I think you are mad. Yes, all of you. The news – surely you must realize by now what is going to happen. War, destruction, everywhere. The whole world. And you do nothing, nothing. Someone must do . . .' They could hear him coughing.

Then, 'Hostages to fortune, that's the sort of nonsense you understand. Your children are hostages to fortune. They can start again when you lot have destroyed yourself and your world. You should thank me. You should . . .'

Silence for a few seconds. Then the voice spoke for the last time :

'GET CLEAR. TURN YOUR HEADS. DO NOT WATCH. LIE DOWN. I AM GOING TO TAKE OFF NOW. I AM GOING TO TAKE OFF NOW. COVER YOUR HEADS AND GUARD YOUR EYES. THE CHILDREN ARE . . .'

There was the noise of an express train, then twenty express trains, then a tearing shriek of blasting jets. The great craft seemed bathed in fire. It rose slowly, slowly, and the legs entered the body. The fury of the noise increased. The people clutched their heads. Their mouths were O's, but their screaming could not be heard above the huge outcry of the ship. It rose, still slowly, then faster. Then much faster.

People raised their heads and looked. They saw a dwindling point of fire in the sky, heard the rumbling express-train noise booming and re-echoing among their familiar little hills.

It was gone.

Chapter 5

The Flight Lieutenant hadn't moved. He lay at full length on the floor, his head in Sandra's lap. His face was glazed with sweat. His colour was red, yet bloodless.

'You're ill,' said Sandra softly. She touched his forehead. It was moist and burning. She removed her finger quickly. She disliked the feeling of his skin. She could not help staring at the spots on his face: spots like tiny water blisters. She had never seen anything like them before.

He moved and spoke. 'Stand clear! Get well clear!' he said, in the harsh, loud tone he had used only minutes before when they were still on Earth, still in Little Mowlesbury.

'Get that old man away!' said the Flight Lieutenant, loudly.

Tony came to. He blinked, shook his head, and got to his feet, staring. 'What happened?' he said. 'Where – Oh! That Flight Lieutenant! He done it to us then!' He said all this quite calmly, then looked dully at Sandra with his mouth open. He was still dazed.

The other children stirred, and one by one awakened. Spadger was quickly and tidily sick in a newspaper. The rest were silent and wide-eyed. They formed a ring round Sandra and the Flight Lieutenant. They stood silent, some of them pressing their hands against their ears.

'If your ears hurt, open your mouth wide,' said Brylo. 'As if you were yawning. It's the change of pressure.' Some of them did, and Sandra thought to herself that their gaping faces above her made the whole thing even more mad and unbelievable and terrifying. They were in the sky, in space, rocketing further and further away from home. Yet all around her were the untidy, familiar faces of Tiddler and Spadger and Di and Tony and Brylo, all of them framed in the tidy, unfamiliar cabin of the spaceship or flying saucer – what *was* its proper name? What *were* they doing in it? *Why?* How *long?*

Violently, the Flight Lieutenant jerked upright, pressed his hands to his ears, opened his mouth and appeared to scream silently. His eyes lost their vacant look. He shook his head once and spoke – this time in his ordinary voice.

'That was a shocking take-off. I'm sorry. I flaked out early on, I think – passed out cold. I don't know how many g's we hit – what I mean is, we came up too fast – I'm sorry! Help me up.'

They did so. And Sandra thought, why does he need help to get up? What's wrong with him?

They put the Flight Lieutenant in an aluminium-framed, padded chair in front of a console of instruments. On all four sides of the crowded space around him were more instruments, more dials, more screens, more gauges, meters, warning lights, counters, knobs, pointers, handles, displays.

'I want to go home now,' said Beauty, bravely. But her eyes were swimming.

'Oh, Beauty!' cried Sandra, hugging her. 'And I don't understand *any* of it!' She burst into tears.

Suddenly all the children were talking at once, shouting questions and threats and demands and more questions . . .

'SHUT UP!' yelled the Flight Lieutenant. 'SHUT UP, SHUT UP, SHUT UP!'

They stared at him, silent. His face was scarlet except for his nostrils, which were bone-white. They could see the pulses pounding in his temples and the tiny things like water blisters standing out on his face.

'I'm sorry,' said the Flight Lieutenant. 'Or have I said that before? Yes, I have. But I'm not. Not sorry, I mean. I mean, I'm sorry to drag you away from your homes like this – well, that's putting it mildly – but it had to be done. That should be obvious enough even to a child.'

He mopped his forehead with a handkerchief.

'No offence. You're all children, I know. That's the whole point, you see. It's *because* you're children – can't you understand?'

He faltered and stopped. 'Say something, someone!' prayed Sandra. 'Say something, do something, make him take us back home!'

It was Tony who spoke. His crow's voice hit at the Flight Lieutenant.

'You're off your flippin' nut, mister airman,' he said, his voice hard and jeering. 'You made a mess of getting us up here and you're making a mess of telling us *why* we're up here. But there's one thing you mustn't make a mess of, and that's getting us down. DOWN. See?'

He poked his head forward so that it almost touched the Flight Lieutenant's face. 'DOWN. Now you're taking us DOWN. See?'

'That's right, you tell him, Tone!' said Di in a nervous scream.

The Flight Lieutenant did not move. Tony put a hand on his shoulder and shook him.

'Hey, MISTER AIRMAN! I want to go DOWN! Get the message? DOWN!'

The Flight Lieutenant's elbows slid forward lazily and his head fell forward with a soft bump on to his arms. Brylo was at his side quickly. He looked hard at the Flight Lieutenant's face, then lifted an eyelid with his finger. 'It's no good, Tony,' he said. 'He's passed out again.'

'Is he dead?' screamed Di.

Chapter 6

They knew from the clock – the only dial they could understand – that two hours had passed since the Flight Lieutenant
had lost consciousness. During that time, they had explored
most of the ship.

It was huge. The control cabin where the Flight Lieutenant lay – white faced, but breathing regularly and cocooned
with blankets – was only a small and still mysterious part
of the whole. A dove-grey corridor from Control led to what
Brylo thought was a navigation room with a single bunk.
Facing it was what appeared to be a Communications or
Radio Room, also with a bunk.

From there on, dove-grey corridors led to rooms that were
increasingly to do with humans and less to do with the ship.
There were, for example, two separate shower rooms, one
with equipment of a sort that Brylo guessed to be connected
with decontamination : if you suffered some sort of injury,
obviously this was the shower you used. Brylo kept this conclusion to himself. He thought he could guess the sort of injury and he did not like his thoughts.

There were also a very small library (the books and maga-
zines, Brylo noted, were all non-technical); a cinema with
twenty seats and a large television screen; a music room with
an excellent record player but no records in the shelves; a
very small gymnasium only partly equipped; a small dormi-
tory and a number of separate cabins with beds; a canteen
seating twenty, a small and well furnished dining-room seating six and a gleaming, elaborate kitchen.

'Do themselves well, whoever they are,' sniffed Di.

'Let's find out how well,' said Tony. 'We got to eat . . .'

Brylo began to prod knobs one by one in a methodical fashion. Tony said, 'Oh, for flip's sake!' and pressed all the knobs at once. It worked. Pilot lights lit, electricity hummed. Tony kept pressing the knobs. A hatch opened and an egg salad on a plate appeared. Then another and another.

'Dish 'em out,' said Tony grandly.

'I haven't got a fork or a knife,' Beauty complained.

'Look till you flippin' find one,' said Tony. Beauty opened the drawer nearest her. It was filled with knives and forks.

'Oh, thank you, Tony!' she said. She looked at him wonderingly and he could not help grinning. She smiled back and decided that Tony was very nice.

'You are clever, Tony,' she said. As she ate, she kept her eyes on him, admiring him.

The girls were busy. 'This hotplate's hot,' said Di.

'Find out which switch,' said Tony.

'The water boiler's full and the water's getting hot . . .'

'Find some tea or cocoa and bung it in and brew up, then.'

'Look, this knob makes cornflakes come out . . .'

'Well, don't stand there. Find flippin' BOWLS.'

They ate, left the dishes, and went on exploring.

They found a wine cupboard full of wine bottles, all full.

They found, low down in the ship, a whole gallery of corridors and doors, all marked DANGER. Behind most of the doors, they could hear the sounds of power – the hum and whine and roar of the things that drove the ship.

'I'll take a look,' said Tony, still chewing at a hard-boiled egg.

'Don't, Tony,' said Brylo, very seriously.

Tony stopped, turned and faced Brylo. He finished chewing his egg and then asked, 'Who's the boss here, Brylo boy? You or me?'

'Don't go in there, Tony, you've no idea what . . .'

'I said, who's boss?'

The rest watched silently. Di sidled up to stand by Tony. He stared at Brylo.

'It's nothing to do with who's boss,' said Brylo. 'I don't care who's boss . . .'

'Well, I do and it's me. I'm boss. All right, Brylo boy?'

'Just don't go messing about behind those doors . . .'

'You never know with old Brylo boy,' said Tony to Di, turning away from Brylo. 'Never know whether he's all brown, or brown with a yellow streak.'

Di gave a scream of laughter. Some of the others sniggered weakly. Brylo swallowed, blinked, racked his brains for a reply and found none. It did not help when Beauty slipped her hand into his and confided, 'I'm glad Tony is the boss, aren't you?'

But at least Tony did not open any of the doors marked DANGER.

Chapter 7

The Tiddler came running up the corridor. 'He's still asleep, Tony,' he said. 'I took a good look at him and he's no worse.'

'Did you make sure his blankets were still on him?'

'He'd hardly moved, Tony . . .'

'I didn't ask if he'd moved, did I? I asked about his flippin' *blankets*. You want to wash your ears out. And there's something else you can do. You can stop calling me Tony. You can call me Captain. That goes for all of you. Right?'

'Aye, aye, Cap'n,' said Tiddler, giving a nautical salute and rolling his eyes. There was some friendly laughter.

Tony walked over to Tiddler and hit him twice almost in the same movement, once with the back of his hand and once with the front. Tiddler's eyes popped with surprise, then his face puckered and he began to cry. 'You hurt my *ear*, you rotten idiot!' he yelled and ran at Tony. Spadger caught Tiddler's arm and pulled him aside.

It was just as well. Tony's face was set in hard fury. His fists were clenched, his mouth twisted. They were used to his rages and his outbursts, but they had never seen him like this.

'IT'S NOT FLIPPIN' FUNNY!' he shouted.

'We weren't laughing, Tony, honest,' said Billy Bason.

'You laughed when I said call me Captain! You did, I saw you!' shouted Tony. 'And *you* laughed! And *you*!' He jabbed his finger at Sandra and Spadger. They turned to Brylo for support, but he was looking down at the ground.

Brylo was thinking. The Flight Lieutenant sick, with an illness Brylo could not place; themselves in a flying saucer, which might be heading for an infinity of space or for a head-on smash against the Earth, the Moon – anywhere; and Tony – Tony already beginning to act like a little Adolf Hitler. He wondered miserably if Tony had ever heard of Adolf Hitler and then pulled himself together and tried to think of something more to the point. But once again, Tony got there first; suddenly he was all smiles and friendliness.

'All right ! Come on Tiddler, turn it up – you'll frighten Tich here !'

Beauty smiled at him uncertainly.

'All I ask is, just remember one thing. All of you. Someone's got to be boss. It better be me. So just you call me, Captain. Captain. OK? Captain ! Simple enough, isn't it? I'm your Captain. I'll see you through so long as no one interferes. OK, Brylo?' Brylo did not look up. 'Good boy, that's my Brylo ! Now, where were we? Exploring the ship, that's where. All right, follow me !'

They found the biggest room of all.

It was positioned right away from the 'Danger' parts and well away from Control. It was a beautifully equipped lounge, with a conference table in an annexe and a number of softly upholstered easy chairs. There was a drinks cabinet, a TV screen with a small console of controls in front of it and a hatch to serve food. There were two antique globes, one of the stars and the other, of Earth, beautifully restored to bring the map up to date. There were provisions for wall displays, a little square window denoting a cinema projection booth and everything else needed for comfort, discussion, work or relaxation.

'It's like those great Board Rooms you see in the films !' said Billy Bason. 'You know, Big Tycoon !'

'Number 10 Downing Street, Space version !' said Di, throwing her legs in the air from one of the deepest chairs.

'What do you make of it, Brylo boy?' said Tony, being consciously affable.

'Di's right – that's what I think,' said Brylo shortly.

'What do you mean? Do you mean that ...'

'Be all right for that perishing little Ashley. Just his style!' said Di maliciously.

'Where is Ashley?' said Sandra.

'Heh! That's right, he came aboard with us! Where is he?' said Tony.

'Anyone seen him?'

'He didn't come exploring with us, I don't remember seeing him after we left the Flight Lieutenant ...'

'And he's not with the Flight Lieutenant or I'd have seen him,' said Tiddler.

'You, you and you – go and find him!' said Tony pointing at Spadger, Billy and Sandra. He stretched himself out in a chair and added, 'Go on! Get moving!'

Spadger and Billy looked at each other and shrugged. 'All right, Tony,' said Spadger.

'Not *Tony*,' said Tony. 'It's *Captain*. You say, "All right, *Captain*!" Remember?'

When they came back from the search, Billy and Spadger were laughing and even Sandra could not help smiling.

'You'll never guess where we found him, Ton ... Captain!' said Billy.

'He was in that little room where all the radio bits are, you know ...'

'The Communications room ...' said Sandra.

'And he'd got himself some blankets and he'd made them up all very tidily into a proper bed ...'

'Like a nest!' said Spadger.

'... And he'd got himself all burrowed in among the gear in there, with his dressing-gown hung up on the wall all tidy and his slippers ...'

'... Bunny-rabbit slippers!'

'... His slippers on the floor side by side, and we came in and he half woke up and you'll never guess what he said, Tony!'

'*Captain.* Well, go on, tell us, then.'

'He said, "*I'm ready for my drinkie, Mummy*"!'

Billy and Spadger clutched each other and roared. Everyone laughed except Tony. He said, 'My drinkie, Mummy. It makes you sick. Flippin' *sick* !'

And everyone stopped laughing.

Chapter 8

The Flight Lieutenant regained consciousness at five o'clock in the morning. Sandra was awakened by his murmurings and got up from her improvised bed beside him. He opened his eyes. Sandra said, 'Are you all right? Can you hear me? Do you want something?'

He looked at her in a dull, tired way, and replied, 'I think I'm all right. Help me to sit up. That's better. I've got to talk to *you, all of you*.'

'I'd better get Tony, he's the Captain.'

'Is he all right?' said Spadger, waking up. He, too, had made his bed in Control.

'Go and get Tony. You know where he is,' said Sandra.

'I know where Tony is – pardon, *Captain* Tony,' said Spadger bitterly, disentangling himself from his blankets. 'He's in the Captain's Cabin. The Executive Suite. Big Tycoon. Oh well, I'll go and get him. Are you really better?' he asked the Flight Lieutenant. 'You look a bit better anyhow. I'll go and get Tony.'

'I must look like hell,' said the Flight Lieutenant miserably.

Brylo came in and, without speaking, put his hand on the Flight Lieutenant's forehead and took his pulse. 'I think you're a bit better than you were, but you don't look too good.'

'Don't want the rest to see me like this,' mumbled the Flight Lieutenant. He got a comb out and began to use it.

As he combed his hair, great tufts of it came out.

Sandra gave a strangled 'Oh!' and began to cry quietly. Brylo put a hand to her shoulder and said to the Flight Lieu-

35

tenant, 'Listen ! Talk quickly before the others come – Sandra here will be all right, she's got sense. What's wrong with you? What have you got?'

'Do you know what radiation means?' said the Flight Lieutenant. His voice shook.

'Yes. You mean atomic radiation. Radiation sickness? Yes, I know.'

'Well, I know too. I've learned the hard way. Pretty, isn't it?' There was a pause. 'You seem a pretty sensible kid. And you too, Sandra. I don't know so much about the others. That boy with all the blond hair, there's something wrong there, you'll have to watch him . . .'

'Your sickness,' said Sandra.

'Oh, yes. It's radiation sickness all right. What the service calls a self-inflicted injury in my case. I asked for it, I got it. Over-gunned the nuclear motor when I took the ship. Too much for the shielding to take . . .' Once again, the Flight Lieutenant seemed to come to a full stop, as if he had been run down.

'But how? When?' Brylo pressed him.

'Here. In this ship. And recently. A matter of days.'

Tony came in, wide awake and there were sounds of the approach of the others. The Flight Lieutenant hid the comb under his blankets.

'What's going on?' Tony demanded. 'You got up, Flight Lieutenant. Why did you do that? Are you better or what?'

The Flight Lieutenant looked at Brylo and gave a twisted smile. 'Get all the children in here, Tony,' he said. 'I've got to talk to all of you. Immediately. There isn't much time. Oh, Lord, I think I'm going to be sick again.'

'Sandra, get the kids. All of them. Even flippin' Ashley.'

At least, thought Brylo, Tony has got sense. He knows when to act fast. I wish I did.

By the time the children had assembled, the Flight Lieutenant was back from the bathroom. He looked very ill indeed. He kept putting his hand to his face as if to make sure it was there. He would speak, and then touch himself experimentally, almost as if he were trying to assure himself of his own existence.

'All right,' he began, 'First of all, why you're here. You're here because I brought you here. No one else is involved. Only me and you. I brought you here because I think there's going to be another war, one heck of a blow-up – the final war. A complete mess. Nothing left of anything. Of course, I could be wrong...'

'He could be wrong!' jeered Tony.

'Wait a minute!' said Brylo. 'What about that news flash? You remember, when we were all under the ship on the meadow. You borrowed a transistor set and ...'

'Oh, *that*!' said the Flight Lieutenant wearily. 'Bit of play-acting, that's all, to persuade your parents to let you come aboard. There wasn't any more news, still the same old nonsense about what *we* said and what *they* said. Threats and counter-threats, the same old rigmarole ...'

He lost concentration and touched his face. Then he seemed to gain a spurt of energy.

'But you can't blot out a whole world!' he cried. 'Or even if you can, something must be saved. You, *you* must be saved! You can start again, your children could rebuild life on Earth. Or perhaps they couldn't I don't know.'

'Rebuild it?' said Brylo. 'But you've just said that the world might be destroyed! You can't rebuild a lump of radio-active clinker!'

'Did I say Earth?' said the Flight Lieutenant. 'I suppose I did. Habit. What I mean is you could rebuild human civilization ...'

'On this ship? But ...'

'No, not on this ship, this is only a means of transport.'

'Then where?' Brylo demanded.

'Oh,' said the Flight Lieutenant, touching his face, 'on the moon, I suppose ...'

The children gasped.

'He supposes!' said Tony, bitterly.

Brylo interrupted him. 'You mean on the Moon Station? But they've only been up there just under a year, they've only just started!'

'Oh, they'd make room for you!' said the Flight Lieutenant. 'That's the whole point! You're all kids – children. Everyone loves children, even that shower of politicians and generals and lunatics on Earth! Don't you see, the whole world will be made to see reason now you're up here! You're hostages! Hostages to the whole world – to world peace! They'll kill a thousand soldiers here and ten thousand civilians there and not even notice. But children! That's different. Oh, they'll take notice of you all right!'

'Get him!' said Tony wryly, biting his thumbnail. 'Just the right bloke to be cast adrift in space with! And all because he thinks there might be a war ...'

'Are we really going to the moon?' said Beauty, huge-eyed.

'We'll be lucky if we get to Southend with *him*,' said Tony.

'Never mind that, there are far more important things,' said Brylo. 'Listen, Flight Lieutenant. Are you listening? Tell us what we've got to *do*! Tell us how long the engines will run, how much food there is, how much oxygen if that's what we're breathing, how to navigate, how to get in touch with Earth!'

'He's not hearing,' said Sandra quietly. Gently, she tugged at the Flight Lieutenant's sleeve. He just sat slumped, his hand to his face.

'Get something wet and cold and put it on his head,' said Tony.

'Look!' said Brylo. 'Let's see what we *do* know. We know that almost everything he told us when he landed was lies. He could take off and he did. There hasn't been an ultimatum about peace and war, they're still arguing. He's only a Flight Lieutenant, yet he was alone in this ship – so he must have kidnapped it, just as he kidnapped us.'

'He didn't tell us what the ship is for,' said Spadger.

'Well, that's obvious, isn't it? It's a special ship, probably a one-off thing, for important people ...'

'It's a VIP funk-hole, if you want to know!' said the Flight Lieutenant, without raising his head. 'It was built to get the government big-wigs and the top brass away from the bombs they're preparing to drop! It's a technological marvel, furnished in the best possible taste throughout with soft seats for a limited number of distinguished backsides! It's the cleverest, stinkingest, most highly advanced funk-hole the world has ever seen – although I suppose they've got just the same things in Russia and America and ...'

'Never mind all that!' yelled Tony. 'Just tell us how long it will run, how to make it go, how it all *works*!'

The Flight Lieutenant lifted his flushed, perspiring head and stared at Tony.

'Me tell you?' he gasped. 'Me? The humble dogsbody Flight Lieutenant?' He broke into a coughing laugh. 'Me tell you how the thing works? Look, sonny, I got radiation burns that will kill me in a week learning what I learned, and I don't know *anything*!'

Chapter 9

In fact, the Flight Lieutenant knew quite a lot.

For the next two days, Sandra nursed him and Brylo patiently cross-questioned him, noting down everything that seemed significant. He did this for his own benefit and also for the others in case anything happened to him.

Water, Food, he wrote. More than enough packaged and prepared meals for a month. Plenty of food in tins and cold store. Plenty of water and apparently a regenerating unit to make more.

Oxygen: uncertain, but probably enough. All oxygen cylinders believed full (check by tapping, full cylinders gave different note from empty). Ships own Carbon monoxide recycling unit – performance not known. In operation now? How is Oxygen content read and stabilized? Instrument somewhere? ?

Lighting: electric power: available indefinitely.

Power: ship has three motors, one more or less a rocket drive for maximum take-off and counter-thrust when landing, the others 'space' drives to propel ship. These two nuclear.

FLIGHT LIEUTENANT GOT HIS RADIATION DOSE FROM ENTERING 'DANGER' ROOM CONTAINING NUCLEAR-DRIVE MOTOR: ALSO FROM RUNNING THESE ENGINES ABOVE THE SAFETY LIMIT INDICATED ON THE DRAWING ATTACHED. READINGS ON THESE DIALS MUST NOT EXCEED LIMITS MARKED – FLIGHT LIEUTENANT DID NOT UNDERSTAND AND EXCEEDED LIMITS. RADIATION SHIELDS INEFFECTIVE WHEN LIMITS EXCEEDED BEWARE OF THIS.

Take-off procedure: Flight Lieutenant gave maximum 'boost' from rocket-type motors (probably unnecessary to use maximum) and also nuclear space drive early on. Thus violent take-off? Less power needed?

Landing: same as above, but Flight Lieutenant says easier to judge power for landing, you can watch ground coming up. OBVIOUSLY ROCKET DRIVE IS THE ONE THAT MATTERS WHEN YOU ARE ANYWHERE NEAR EARTH. CONTROLS: SEE DIAGRAM.

Navigation: not understood. Flight Lieutenant believes craft can be navigated only from inside, not from Earth (because craft used to escape from destroyed Earth??).

Vision: Flight Lieutenant has shown me how to work Near Vision, but cannot understand long-distance apparatus. Does it exist? YOU CAN SEE IMMEDIATELY AROUND YOU FROM SHIP, BUT NOT OVER LONG DISTANCES. NO WINDOWS IN SHIP.

Controls: SEE DIAGRAM.

Communications: Flight Lieutenant says ship capable of receiving and sending radio, and able to receive TV but cannot work the sets, which seem dead??????

State of ship: the ship was kept in almost 100 per cent readiness always. When the Flight Lieutenant stole it, it was fully fitted out except Communications equipment not working???? Flight Lieutenant thinks missing items, if any, would most likely be very minor – e.g., luxuries, toilet items. (Thus no records for music room??)

First Aid: Medical Room with Red Cross on door. DO NOT TOUCH CONTENTS OF SMALL TIN BOX WITH PADLOCK – DANGEROUS DRUGS.

Showers – the medical showers are for people who have got a dose of radiation or think they have. HAVE TAPED INSTRUCTIONS FOR USE TO DOOR. DO NOT REMOVE.

As Brylo made his notes, he acted on them methodically, putting first things first – oxygen, because that was the very air they breathed; water, because he knew that they could live longer without food than without water; and so on. He soon discovered the oxygen instruments, for example, and noted that both his reserves and the oxygen balance inside the ship were completely satisfactory; apparently the balance was maintained automatically, for the dial needles barely shifted.

He inspected the food stores with Sandra and discovered the secrets of the egg salads. There were considerable stores of ready prepared foods delivered from a deep-freeze electric conveyor belt with a push-button programming and actuating system. To Brylo, this seemed unnecessarily elaborate. So did the electric and electronic trickeries and gimmicks of the great lounge. He began to understand the resentment that had invaded the Flight Lieutenant's mind. The ship was indeed a sort of scientific jewel-case, far too generously filled with jewels.

He worked with increasing urgency at his notes, for the Flight Lieutenant was weakening. He was constantly vomiting. His temperature was 104. The water blisters multiplied, joined, made islands, countries and continents on his face. Brylo preferred not to think about his hair, and what happened when he combed it, or even tossed his head on his pillow.

Brylo made another note:

Waste matter: human and kitchen waste products automatically voided from ship via toilets, waste-disposal units etc, with very slight and unimportant loss of air. IF SOMETHING BIG MUST BE EJECTED FROM SHIP, USE AIRLOCK IN EXIT COMPARTMENT.

He finished writing this and looked at the Flight Lieutenant for a long time, pitying him. Then he picked up his ballpoint and added a footnote to what he had written:

HOW MUCH AIR IS LOST WHEN AIRLOCK IS USED?

Chapter 10

It was night again (or was it? Only the clocks told them
when it was night and when it was day). The children prepared to go to their beds.

Sandra combed out her long, heavy brown plait; plaited
it again; looked in the mirror and wished yet again that her
face was not so broad, not so 'jolly'. She thought of her
favourite pop star, Cindy Sue, and wished for the millionth
time that she, Sandra, could have that almond-shaped face,
the long-lashed dark eyes, the curling mouth with huge
dimples at each corner, the glinting, sweeping wave of hair . . .

'You wouldn't want to sound like her, anyhow!' she con-
soled herself. And she began to imitate Cindy Sue's hiccough-
ing whine when she sang 'Don't Mean It, Baby'.

'You are making a funny noise!' said Beauty.

'Come here and I'll do your hair and make you look smashing,' Sandra replied. She took a firm hold of the thick, honey-
coloured, silken waves and parted them down the middle to
reveal Beauty's tender, slender neck. She touched the gold
down on it with a fingertip and said, 'Your neck's too thin
to hold your head up, did you know that?'

'My head will go all wobbly, won't it?' gurgled Beauty,
delighted with the idea. She began to murmur 'wibble . . .
wobble . . .' in time with the strokes as Sandra put aside the
brush and took up a comb. Sandra thought of home.

She thought of the hundreds, thousands of times that her
mother had combed her hair for her just as she was combing
Beauty's. She remembered how she had sometimes tugged and
complained – 'Oh, Mum-mee!' –and how her mother used to

say. 'Eh, be quiet! Eh, be still!' She remembered learning to make her own plait — practising for hours in the kitchen, with the sun streaming through the little green-painted window with its red and white check curtain. She remembered the dishmop and the lazy buzzing of a fly and the hollyhocks outside and the enormous box of matches with a ship on it that was cheaper than buying lots of little boxes. She remembered her father smacking her hand when he found her playing with the matches and how she shouted, 'I hate you! I hate you!'

'It's this ship I hate,' thought Sandra. 'I didn't even know what hate meant when I was a little girl. I know now. It's this ship.'

'Am I done now?' said Beauty. 'Am I smashing?'

'You look like a bunch of flowers in a red ribbon!' said Sandra, using the old Mowlesbury words that her mother had used to her.

Beauty ran from her and dived straight on to her bed, flailing her legs. 'Smashing, smashing, smashing!' she yelled.

'Don't say that word any more, lovie, I'm sick of it,' said Sandra.

'Why, what does it mean?'

I could give her more than one answer, thought Sandra, and shivered suddenly as she tucked Beauty in.

Spadger, Billy Bason and the Tiddler shared a room. It wasn't a bad sort of room. The bunks were alloy, the walls light grey, and there were pipes and cables running over their heads across the ceiling. Set into one wall was a metal plate with a grille at the top from which came clicking noises at regular intervals. They had made these noises into part of their play. They called themselves 'The Three From Outer Space'.

'Check the airlock,' said Spadger. Billy Bason and the Tiddler seized the door and, grunting with pretended exertion, forced it closed. They waited for a few seconds, and sure enough – *Click!* went the thing behind the panel in the wall.

'Airlock closed!' said Tiddler.

'Proceed to count-down!' said Billy Bason.

'All right men ... awaiting synchronization ...' said Spadger, examining an imaginary wrist watch.

Click! went the thing behind the panel.

'Ten ... Nine ... Eight ... Seven ... Six ... Five ... Four ... Three ... Two ... One ... BLAST OFF!'

They flung themselves on their bunks and covered their heads with their hands. They made jet howls that got louder and louder and higher and higher, until ...

Click!

'Cut all jets! Switch to Spacedrive! Bring in Anti-grav when you hear the signal! ...'

Click!

'Antigrav operational! All right, men, we're on our own. Us against *Them*!'

'Can you hear anything, Brains?'

'I – thought – I – heard ...' said Tiddler, in his metallic 'Brains' voice.

'Herr Oberschnitz?'

'Nein. I am hearing not one thing. Should we the light turn out?' said Spadger.

'Sure thing, men,' said Billy Bason in his voice of Captain Freedom. He switched out the light. 'Reckon if they're going to show, we'll be hearing from them real soon. ...'

Click!

'I wish you'd get another name for yourself, Billy,' said Spadger in his own voice. 'All this "Captain" stuff makes me sick. We've got enough Captains ...'

'One's enough. More than enough.'

'*Captain* Tony. Captain Tony Hoskings. Makes me sick.'

'He's gone off his nut with this Captain lark.'

'He was off his nut before ...'

Click!

'Vot was dot, mein kamerads?' whispered Herr Ober-schnitz.

'Get – your – Ray-guns – ready – for – immediate – action –' said Brains.

'Cool it fellers! Play it real cool . . . !' murmured Captain Freedom.

Click!

Tony pressed a button and an egg salad came out. He ate the egg, dipping it in the blob of mayonnaise, then threw the rest down a disposal chute. Then he made his way back to the biggest room of all – the beautifully equipped lounge. The Captain's room. His room.

It was time for bed and he felt sleepy. Good and sleepy, sleepy and good. Not sick at all – yet the bottle of wine on the table was almost half empty. Tony decided he must have a pretty strong head. He could drink like a man. A man among boys. He was the only real man on the ship: you couldn't count the Flight Lieutenant any more . . .

'You're on the way out, Lieut!' he murmured. 'Ya know that? Finished! Washed up! Believe me, man, you're on the way out!'

He let himself fall into a big armchair and hardly felt the pain as one of the arms thumped into his ribs. 'Not a good landing, man!' he said to himself, and caught himself chuck-ling.

This surprised him. He sat bolt upright in the chair and thought hard. Why had the chair hit him? Because he had fallen into it untidily. Why had he fallen into it untidily? Because he had drunk nearly half a bottle of wine.

'Moron!' he said. 'You're the Captain, remember?'

He poured the rest of the wine down a disposal chute and let the bottle go too.

'You're in command,' he reminded himself.

In command of what? He sat down carefully, and began to work it out. 'Take a roll call,' he instructed himself.

Flight Lieutenant? Dying. No action until he actually died. Brylo? Well under control. Brylo knew when he was licked and Tony had him licked. Sandra? Good girl. She takes care of Beauty and the Lieut. Spadger, Billy Bason, the Tiddler? Like kids at a carnival. No sense, not an idea among the three of them. Kids playing kids' games. Forget them. Ashley? Flippin' mummy's darling. Get Sandra to take care of him, make sure he eats, clean his toofy-woofies.

'What a mob!' he thought. 'What a shower! But they'll do what I tell them. They'll call me Captain or get their heads punched. They admire me, because I know what to do. . . .'

Something was wrong, though. Tony got up from the chair and stood by a table, kicking it gently with his big toe. What exactly *were* they doing? Heading for the moon, or for outer space, or back to earth, or what? And did it matter? As long as he was boss, everything was all right. It was being boss, being Captain, that mattered. They never let him be boss at home. The teachers were always picking on him at school, he was never boss there. Now he was boss. It wasn't *his* fault if he couldn't make the ship go where it should go, wherever that was. It wasn't *his* fault that he couldn't work the controls – if the Flight Lieutenant couldn't, and brainy Brylo couldn't, why expect him to be able to? Why pick on him? Why blame him?

Suddenly, he felt a little sick. The wine! Better go to bed, it was nearly twelve. He lay down on the long couch and pulled a blanket over him, then realized that he would have to get up again to turn out the lights. Flippin' lights! He closed his eyes to see if he could go to sleep with them on, but the room seemed to lurch and swing. He sat up.

'Where was I?' he said out loud. That's right, he was taking a roll call – ticking off everybody on board. He started to go through it again. Had he remembered everyone?

'Remember me?' said the piercing voice of Di.

She stood in the doorway looking at him with her head on one side.

'You keep out of here,' said Tony. 'My room. Captain's cabin.'

Di ignored him. 'You've gone white!' she said. 'Your face is all *white*! What have you been at?'

'Flippin' – clear – OUT!' said Tony. But the effort brought a wave of sickness to his throat and he gasped, disgustedly.

'I'll get a cold cloth ...'

'Don't bother yourself. Flippin' clear out.'

'You've been at that wine, that's what it is!' said Di, bustling out.

Tony could have killed her for knowing. He propped himself up on one arm and was about to shout at her when the wave of sickness came back, worse than ever.

Di flounced back into the room with a wet cloth. She sat down beside him on the couch and put it on his forehead. 'You've been a soppy old Captain, haven't you?' she said. Tony writhed, but the cold cloth felt wonderful.

'Can't say I blame you,' she went on. 'I mean, it's a big responsibility, isn't it? Being Captain, I mean ...'

She turned the cloth. It felt even better.

'You take care of them,' said Di, speaking softly for once, 'and I'll take care of you. Right?'

Tony didn't answer. But he let her stay.

Chapter 11

Brylo put down his ballpoint and rubbed his forehead with both hands. He looked again at the clock: almost midnight. No, he thought, almost twelve. There is no night, no day, up here. But day or night, I should go to sleep. I cannot work any more.

He lay down on a bunk in an annexe of Control. The bunk was of alloy and pulled from the wall. It had a plastic foam mattress with a pillow shaped in it. He wondered how much the whole thing weighed. Very little. Probably a pound or so. Ingenious . . .

And comfortable. Tomorrow, he would look more carefully at the radio console in Control. Obviously their immediate needs were taken care of – food, water, air. If only they could communicate! If only they could get in touch with Earth! But the Flight Lieutenant was delirious. And when he had been fairly normal and able to speak rationally, he had made it quite clear that he understood very little of the functions of the apparatus in Control.

Brylo decided that he must yet again go right over every item in Control, concentrating on its radio and television equipment – the possible links with Earth. But should he also take a look at the Communications room? No, don't bother. If *you* were designing a craft like this, he told himself, you would put everything you needed in one place, in one room. So Control was like a ship's bridge. Everything the Captain and the senior officers might need was controllable from the bridge. The Communications room was merely a specialist department – like, say, a telephone exchange. To use a telephone, you don't go to the telephone exchange: you merely lift up your receiver and dial. So what he had to do was to master the dialling system, so as to speak. And that should operate from Control . . .

The bed was very comfortable. Brylo realized, with a dim pleasure, that he was falling asleep. He encouraged his mind to form pictures. Obligingly, it came up with an old cigarette card – a slightly blurred picture of the bridge of the Queen Mary, with a beef-faced portly Captain standing in front of a shining brass binnacle, a sailor at the wheel and two officers in the background. What were the other cards in the series? Were they all to do with Captains?

His half-asleep mind presented him with another cigarette card – Captain George Eyston, holder of the World Land Speed Record in . . . in . . . When? And had George Eyston been a Captain, or had he got it all wrong? He mused, drowsily and pleasantly.

Suddenly his mind switched tracks and Tony's face was right in front of him, jeering. Captain Tony!

Brylo jerked and sat half upright. Then he forced himself to lie down and clear his mind.

But his mind would not clear itself. Tony appeared again and Brylo resolutely switched him off by thinking of home. What was on his bedside table the night the ship landed? Think of that, he told himself. Memory training. Pelmanism. Remember each item . . .

There were, almost certainly, his green fountain pen and his maths homework because he had been getting ready to work in bed. Also a glass of water – the fluted tumbler. Also a stick of chewing gum. Also *The Adventures of Sherlock Holmes*, which he had been saving for later. He could now picture the top of his bedside table with complete accuracy. Good!

But his tired brain would not hold the picture: it slipped. It fell away, downwards, and became smaller as if he were

50

looking at it down a chimney through a telescope. The table was tiny now, a long way below him. And now it was slipping away and away (or was he rising faster and faster above it?) and he could see the house and the garden and the trees and then the whole village, dimly in the dusk.

Faster still! Now it was like looking down a well at a miniature village, a miniature world – a world in a fish-bowl! He saw that, connecting him and the world, was a gossamer-fine filament like a spider's web, a filament that must not be broken.

He was in space, infinite space, and there was blue-blackness all about him. A million miles down, the tiny world slowly twisted and spun at the end of his filament. As long as the filament held! ...

Then almost total darkness. The world had dwindled to nothing, it was gone. He peered into the darkness, seeking it, following the still-taut line of the glinting filament that connected him to it.

Then the filament loosened, rippled, floated aimlessly in the void.

Uneasily, Brylo slept.

Chapter 12

Ashley had long since crawled into his solitary nest in the Radio Communications room and gone to bed. But he was not asleep.

He lay in the neat bed he had made for himself of three blankets and his woolly dressing-gown. His bunny-rabbit slippers were neatly placed side by side within reach. His comb lay by a folded handkerchief (which he was trying not to use, so that it would keep clean) on the ledge of an insanely complicated console of communications equipment under which he had burrowed to make his bed. His hair was combed and he lay on his back with his hands folded outside the coverlets. He was ready.

'I'm in bed, Mummy!' he called softly.

He waited for a few moments, then said, 'Yes, I *am* in bed. And everything's put away tidily.'

He waited again.

'Can I have my hot drinkie now, Mummy?'

He waited and waited. If he kept still enough, surely something would happen? Something nice? Surely Mummy would come up the stairs, step by step, carefully and surely, bearing his nice hot drink? He waited.

Mummy didn't come.

Ashley rolled over in bed and buried his face in his pillow. He clenched his plump, clean fists and tried not to cry. He succeeded and felt proud of himself. He sat up in bed.

By the dim blue glow from two little lights on the console, he could distinguish a shape that puzzled him for a moment until he remembered what it was: earphones. They lay on a shelf. He got out of bed and picked them up, turning them over in his hands. The earpieces were heavily padded with foam-plastic mouldings. He wondered if they would be comfortable and if wearing them would help him sleep. He tried them on. They felt very nice.

Then he had a better idea. At home, they had a radio set and Daddy understood all about radios. Perhaps – he was not very clear about this – perhaps if he plugged the earphones in somewhere, he would hear Mummy?

He got out of bed and switched on a little light that illuminated the console and a desk in front of it. He examined the jack-plug at the end of the earphones' cable and looked for a hole it would fit. The trouble was, that there were so many holes. And Ashley knew how dangerous electricity is – Mummy was always telling him. 'Don't touch the vacuum cleaner, Ashley!' she would cry, 'It could give you a nasty, nasty, shock!' Ashley didn't want a nasty shock.

But then he remembered Daddy saying that if you touched a 'live' electrical mechanism with the back of your fingers and *did* get a shock, your fingers would curl up into a fist *away* from the shock and you would be safe. Whereas if you touched the dangerous thing in the usual way and got a shock, the shock would make your hand clench the thing and you would go on and on getting the shock until there was smoke curling from your hair and –

Ashley shivered and decided to be very, very careful.

He put the earphones on the shelf, picked up the jack-plug and put it in a hole marked CH 3. He then touched the earphones with the back of his fingers. No shock. Gingerly he put the earphones on.

Nothing. Not a sound except the dull plunging of his own pulse.

He took the earphones off, and went through the procedure again and again. CH 1, CH 2, CH 4, PA 1, PA 1 ex, PA 2, PA 2 ex . . .

Nothing.

Then he noticed that all these holes were in a console that did not have a blue light burning. He moved to another console beside it that did have a blue light, and tried again. He plugged into a socket marked COMM 1.

He was successful immediately. As he put the earphones on, he heard the frizzling, crackling, frying sound of 'live' radio.

But only that. After a time, he reached out a trembling hand and began to turn dials. The first dial made no difference to the sound he heard in the earphones. He tried another, then another.

Suddenly his head was almost burst open by a horrifying scream ! – a scream that went on and on. Screaming himself, Ashley tore at the headphones and scrabbled them from his head – then flung himself into bed and drew the blankets over his head.

The earphones lay on the floor, their metal parts glimmering with reflections of blue light. From them came a continuous, unvarying whistle. . . .

Many minutes later, Ashley slowly uncovered his head. His eyes flickered with panic at first, then fixed themselves on the devilish, whistling, blue-glinting thing on the floor.

Chapter 13

The Flight Lieutenant was sitting bolt upright in his disordered bed when Sandra visited him at two o'clock that night.

'Glad you could come, I'm feeling a bit depressed,' he announced cheerfully. His voice was as she had first heard it – confident and racy.

'What's the matter?' Sandra asked him, smiling. It was wonderful to know that he was better – almost back to normal.

'It's the kids I'm worried about,' said the Flight Lieutenant. 'I mean, suppose there *were* another war! Everyone would cop it! Not just the soldiers and fighting men, but even the ordinary men and women. And the kids. Even the politicians might find things a bit umpty,' he said, knowingly. 'But of course, they've always got a way out. Confidentially –' he paused dramatically – 'I happen to know something that very few other men know. It's about the politicians and the top brass. They've got a funk-hole!'

Something cold seemed to crawl up Sandra's back. He's delirious, she thought. He's worse than ever.

'It's a funk-hole in the sky,' said the Flight Lieutenant. 'Right up high! Higher than a kite! Right up there with the Man in the Moon! I say, that's funny! – because it's true, you know!' He laughed, then said, very seriously, 'I say, I'm glad I never married. Aren't you?'

'I'm a bit young,' said Sandra dully.

'Never too young!' cried the Flight Lieutenant, gaily. 'Never too old! I had to make a speech when I was best man at Toby's wedding. Wish 'em all the best and all that rot. You know Toby, don't you?'

'Oh, yes,' lied Sandra.

'The speech was a bit of a flop, really,' continued the Flight Lieutenant. 'Never could do that sort of thing really well – speaking in public and so on. Not the right type, I suppose. Never make a politician, eh? Blasted politicians. All scum! ...' He picked at the blanket gloomily. Sandra wished only that he would stop – that she could go, could escape. But she knew that she must stay with him.

'Old Toby!' said the Flight Lieutenant, raising his head and grinning delightedly. 'He was a case! He really was a boy! You know Toby, don't you?'

'Oh, yes,' said Sandra. 'I know Toby.'

'What a boyo!' said the Flight Lieutenant. 'Do you remember the time when we were all in Flight B at Nestlington, and he got all the fire extinguishers going at once and we all stood round him playing them on him ... And he wrapped a towel round his head and sat in the middle, like a sultan, singing that song...'

'I remember,' said Sandra.

'What *was* that song?' said the Flight Lieutenant, earnestly.

'Roll out the Barrel?' said Sandra.

'No, not Roll out the Barrel. Not *that*. Oh come on, you remember . . . Was it Roll on, Roll on Harvest Moon?'

'That was it,' said Sandra.

'What a boyo, old Toby!' said the Flight Lieutenant. '"Roll on Harvest Moon!"' He hugged his knees ecstatically. 'One of the boys, old Toby. He'd never have made a politician! Not old Toby! Nothing brass-hat about good old Toby!' He began to sing 'Roll on Harvest Moon' in an unmusical voice. He seemed quite happy.

You poor man, thought Sandra. But really, you're not a man at all. Only a little boy trying to escape it all. Blaming the politicians, the brass-hats. Anyone. If only you could *help* us.

'You were talking about the moon,' she began. 'Harvest Moon!' said the Flight Lieutenant, grinning. 'No, the real moon,' said Sandra, leaning forward. 'We're going to the moon, aren't we? In this ship?'

'A flight to the moon on gossamer wings,' sang the Flight Lieutenant. 'Just one of those things.'

'Look, you must concentrate!' said Sandra. 'Listen to me. You brought us out here in this ship. The ship you stole. The funk-hole ship. We're in it now, at this moment, flying in space. We don't know where we're going. We don't know what might happen to us. Try and help us. Tell me what to do to steer the ship.'

'Oh, that!' said the Flight Lieutenant. 'Well, that's a bit of a teaser. A *bit* of a teaser. Rather top secret, you see. Just the least bit teasing, *vous comprenez?*' He gave an easy laugh, a grown-up, sophisticated laugh. He's trying to escape anything difficult, thought Sandra. I'll never get to him.

She moved closer to him and turned a swivelling lamp so that it lit his face better. He looked awful. Most of his hair was gone. His face was a mass of small blisters and all the skin glistened fiercely. His eyes were red rimmed and brilliant. She nerved herself to put her hand on his forehead: it was burning, burning hotter than ever before. She got up.

'Don't go away!' said the Flight Lieutenant cheerily. 'Sit down and have another! Old Toby will be along in a jiffy.'

'I'm going to fetch him,' said Sandra.

She left the room, and felt tears welling up in her eyes and her throat choking. 'Oh, come *on*!' she said to herself. 'None of that!' She went into Brylo's cabin, switched on the light and woke him up. 'The Flight Lieutenant,' she said, 'he's delirious. And getting worse. Brylo, I think he's going to die quite soon.'

Brylo got out of bed quickly, then slowed himself down and stood thinking. 'My notes,' he said.

'But don't you see, we've got to hurry . . .'

'If he's delirious and getting worse, we probably haven't got him for much longer. And he's the only one that can help us. I've got to make him answer at least one question sensibly and I've got to make sure that I ask him the right question . . .'

'Oh, Brylo, you're hopeless !' shouted Sandra, and ran from him. She would have to get Tony. At least Tony would do something.

Brylo looked at his notes for less than thirty seconds. At the end of that time, he knew what he wanted to know. He left the cabin, shut the door, and walked quickly to the Flight Lieutenant's bedside.

'It's me, Brylo,' he said.

'Hi-ho !' said the Flight Lieutenant. 'I thought you were bringing the boyo himself – old Toby ! Where's old Toby?'

'Don't you mean Tony?' said Brylo, uncertainly.

'Don't know any Tony. Toby's the boy we want ! He's the lad to make the party go . . .'

'Flight Lieutenant, listen !' began Brylo. 'You've got to think. You've got to listen and answer my questions. We're on a ship, remember? Like a space ship. You got us all on to it. But we don't know where we're going or how to work the thing . . .'

'Very, ve-e-e-ry confidential,' said the Flight Lieutenant. 'Funk-hole. Where's old Toby? They'd never make a politician out of old Toby !'

Chapter 14

During the whole five minutes that it took Sandra to waken Tony, wash his face with cold water and get him free of the effects of the wine, Brylo fought a losing battle with the Flight Lieutenant. He understood Brylo's questions, but seemed to slide away from them. It was almost as if he were living in two worlds at once: a world of memory and parties and jokes with good old Toby, and the dimmer world of the ship – a world that was nothing like so attractive.

'All right now, Cap?' said Di, who had been helping Sandra.

'Leave me *alone*, you nit,' said Tony, furious and dishevelled.

'Please hurry, Tony . . .' said Sandra.

'All right, all right! Now, tell me again exactly what that flippin' Flight Lieutenant has been saying. And give me that comb.'

Sandra told him again, watching his eyes in the mirror as he combed his mop of strawlike hair. This time, he was taking it all in. She could see the quick, animal intelligence in his eyes. She could see too that he was planning.

'And Brylo the Brains is with him now?' he interrupted her.

'That's right, he's trying to get him to answer just one question – the question he thinks most important.'

'What question?'

'I don't know, how should I know?'

'Where's the Flight Lieutenant's uniform?' said Tony, cutting across her.

'It's in a cupboard in Control, I put it away when . . .'

'Go and get it. Don't let him see you. Go and get it and bring it here. Move!'

Sandra opened her mouth to say, 'But ...' then thought better of it and ran off. She came back immediately with the uniform.

'Out of my way,' said Tony, by way of thanks. He pulled on the trousers, then the tunic. They were much too big for him. 'Doesn't matter,' he murmured, and put on the peaked cap. It fell over his eyes. 'Get some toilet paper,' he ordered. Di brought him several sheets. He folded them into pads and stuffed them into the lining of the cap until it more or less fitted.

'Get that flippin' shaving cream in the aerosol,' he said. Di brought it.

'All right, you know what Scrambled Eggs is? You don't. Flippin' 'eck, you're dumb as they come. Here, give it us ...' He took off the peaked cap, uncapped the aerosol, made a practice line of foam on the table, then very carefully drew a blobby line of foam right round the curved edge of the cap's peak.

'Scrambled egg,' he muttered.

'Tony, please! We've got to ...'

'Belt up!' roared Tony. Then, recovering his temper, he said: 'Look, you told me that Boy Blue – the Flight Lieutenant – is going off his nut; he's gone all jolly and la-di-da, romps with dear old Toby and all that. And you can't snap him out of it. And you told me that Brainy Brylo is down there with him taking notes and doing his sums. And a fat lot of good that'll do. All right, now I'm going to try a dose of scrambled egg. Come on, let's get cracking.'

He walked to the door. Di flew after him cawing, 'What's all this about scrambled egg, what do you mean, scrambled egg?'

Tony merely replied, 'Top Brass. Air Commodore. Big deal. Come on!'

Sandra and Di followed him.

Chapter 15

In the dark corridor, they could hear Brylo's voice and the
Flight Lieutenant's. They heard Brylo say, 'But listen, you
must ...' and the Flight Lieutenant's reply by beginning a
story about what old Toby did in the Mess on Boxing Day.

'Wait!' said Tony, stretching out a uniformed arm to halt
the two girls. 'I want to hear more!'

'Please!' said Brylo. 'Please, Flight Lieutenant, just answer
me one question. Look, I've got to know about the radio.
The radio! Communications! Tell me how to work the
radio ...'

'So that's it!' whispered Tony. 'Good question. Old Brylo's
dead right. Question number one – radio. OK! Now listen ...

'Di, stay here. Don't follow me. Don't show yourself. Don't
make a sound. Just stay here.

'Sandra, you're to go in there,' he whispered in her ear,
'and you're going to turn the light down or arrange it so that
it won't fall on me when I walk in ... and if he asks you any
stupid questions, just say "Toby is coming". Got that?'

'Toby is coming,' repeated Sandra, and began to move
away.

'Wait a minute, you nit!' whispered Tony, grabbing her
arm. 'When you've said that, you've got to say "But he's
got someone with him. Scrambled eggs!" Got that? Right,
say it!'

' "Toby is coming," ' whispered Sandra, ' "But he's got
someone with him. Scrambled eggs!" '

'Sound more frightened about the last bit,' said Tony,
pinching her arm.

61

' "But he's got someone with him ..." ' said Sandra in a frightened whisper.

'Good. Lovely. Now wait until I give you a shove and get in there and do it ... NOW !'

Just as Brylo began speaking again, Tony pushed Sandra. She walked into the cabin. Tony and Di listened.

'Pardon me, old chap !' said the Flight Lieutenant, turning from Brylo to grin at Sandra. '*Que volez-vous, ma chère Mademoiselle?*'

'Hallo,' began Sandra nervously. She walked casually to the single lamp, and turned it so that its reflector faced the wall.

'Just been telling the laddie here about the old days,' said the Flight Lieutenant. 'You ought to hear. Old Toby and I ...'

'Toby is coming !' said Sandra.

'Oh, good show !' said the Flight Lieutenant, delightedly.

'But he's got someone with him,' said Sandra in a significant voice. 'Scrambled eggs !'

The Flight Lieutenant's face showed bewilderment mixed with apprehension. 'Who ...' he began. But at this moment, Tony made his entrance.

By the dim light from the single lamp, even Sandra could have been deceived. Tony's old-young face, with its angular nose linked to a determined mouth by sharp lines, was made ten, twenty, any number of years older, by the peaked cap with its rim of 'scrambled egg' – gold braid – denoting senior rank. The Flight Lieutenant was completely taken in. He struggled uncertainly to his feet and tried to stand to attention.

'Sir ...' he gasped.

Tony stood stock still in the doorway with his chin jutted forward and his hands behind his back, to conceal the tell-tale two rings on the sleeves of the Flight Lieutenant's jacket and also to give himself a still more aggressive, authoritative pose.

'Stand at ease!' he barked, in his hoarse voice. The Flight Lieutenant, swaying, relaxed slightly. Sandra, watching his pitiful face and his weak figure, thought to herself, 'I don't know whether to laugh or cry . . .'

'Your orders are,' said Tony, 'to keep Control in a state of readiness. It's not in that state. It's in the state of a pig-sty.'

'Sir . . .' said the Flight Lieutenant.

'Radio!' barked Tony. 'I want radio contact with Earth. I want it now. Do it!'

The Flight Lieutenant tottered, put his hand to his head and drew it away, dazedly. Then he inspected the moisture on his fingertips.

'Radio!' barked Tony. 'Come on, man, radio!'

The Flight Lieutenant woke up, and staggered towards Control. Brylo slid from the gloom like a shadow and took his elbow to help him. Together they entered Control. Brylo switched on a light. It was brilliant in there after the gloom of the place where the Flight Lieutenant slept. Tony remained in the gloom.

'Radio!' said Tony's hard voice.

The Flight Lieutenant half walked, half staggered, to a console of radio equipment and stretched out a hand to it. The hand wavered.

'But I don't . . .' he began.

'Come on, man!' said the grating voice of Tony.

'You see, sir, I'm General Duties –' said the Flight Lieutenant, turning his head to the voice from the gloom. 'I never really . . .'

'RADIO EARTH,' said Tony, in a voice as cold as a steel hatchet.

'But I shouldn't . . .'

'You're not fooling me!' said Tony. 'You know. I know you know. Do it!'

Again, the Flight Lieutenant touched his head. Then, with growing certainty, he began to flick switches and turn dials. As he worked, he almost sobbed out excuses and denials.

'I'm not a Tech. man,' he said. 'I've only watched them. It was confidential, secret – I shouldn't!' But his hands continued to obey the threat of Tony's presence.

There was a hum from a loudspeaker, then an oscillating whine, then a continuous crackling whine that changed pitch as the Flight Lieutenant made fine adjustments. Once, there was an ear-filling howl that made the Flight Lieutenant turn apologetically and shamefacedly to Tony. Then he turned back again to his work.

'You – boy – come over here,' said Tony to Brylo.

Brylo went to Tony. 'Is he getting anywhere, the great nit?' muttered Tony. 'Can you understand what he's doing?'

'Keep him at it!' whispered Brylo. 'I've memorized every move he's made. You're doing fine! Keep him trying!'

But Tony didn't have to. Suddenly a French voice filled the room! It rattled on, obviously announcing something, and then there was the undulating whine of Moroccan music!

'Get London!' said Tony, his eyes glittering with excitement.

'Yes, sir! London!' said the Flight Lieutenant. Now he was breathing in gasps and sobs. The sweat from his forehead fell, drop by drop, on the dials and meters, on the controls, on his own hands. Suddenly he swung round towards Tony. His face was agonized.

'I can't get it, sir!' he said. 'Not London! Please, sir, I can't get it! There's a whole frequency band missing . . .'

He fell. Brylo and Sandra rushed to him. Tony flung his cap on the ground and stamped with rage. 'Get the perishing nit on his FEET!' he screamed. 'Get him back on that board!'

'Shut up, Tony!' shouted Sandra. 'Can't you see, he's dying. Dying!' She began to cry bitterly.

The Flight Lieutenant moved. 'Frequency band missing,' he said, in a quiet, normal voice. 'Sorry, sir. Not my fault, sir. Slight fault – jack-plug out in Communications room. Not *my* fault, sir. Not me. Don't blame *me*, sir. It's them. The politicians . . .'

He sank back. His breathing became very noisy.

'He's dying,' sobbed Sandra.

Violently, the Flight Lieutenant jerked upright, with his eyes staring.

'Always me!' he yelled. 'Always me! Always the flaming, dogsbody, Flight Lieutenant!' He choked and fought for breath.

'I'M AS GOOD AS YOU ARE!' he screamed. 'GOOD AS ANY OF YOU! GOOD AS THAT STUPID SWINE TOBY! GOOD AS YOU ROTTEN TOP BRASS! GOOD AS YOU FILTHY POLITICIANS!'

He fell back, heavily.

'He's gone,' said Brylo, a minute later.

Chapter 16

Even Tony was shocked, not only by the Flight Lieutenant's death, but by the hysterical attack from Sandra. She beat at him with her fists. She kept repeating that Tony had killed him, murdered him. Tony backed away from her. Brylo tried to comfort her. But it was not until he said, 'You *must* be quiet. Beauty will hear you!' that she was still.

'Listen, Sandra,' said Brylo, 'you are wrong. Tony was right. He did the right thing. The Flight Lieutenant was going to die anyway. But we, all the rest of us, we want to live. And we can live perhaps if we get the radio working. Tony was right! I wish I'd thought of doing what he did. . . .'

'Flippin' right you wish you had!' jeered Tony.

Brylo turned to him and said, very seriously, 'What you did was absolutely right and you were jolly clever to think of it. But there's no need to . . .'

'Who's that?' said Sandra, tensely. 'Footsteps!'

The footsteps came nearer. 'Who's jolly clever?' said Billy Bason's voice, sleepily, from the corridor.

'Who was yelling and crying?' said Spadger.

Tony leapt to his feet. 'It was me that was jolly clever and it's you lot that's staying outside. Git!' And he slammed the door of Control in their faces.

'What about *him*?' said Tony, his back against the door. He flicked a finger towards the body of the Flight Lieutenant. 'Got anything to cover *that* in your notes, eh, Brylo boy?'

'Don't speak like that about him . . .' said Sandra.

'Yes, it's all in my notes,' said Brylo, staring hard at Tony. 'I know what to do. Do you? And did you know that it's the

Captain that reads the burial service? Are you ready for that?'

'I know just what to say about that flippin' ...' Tony began, when Sandra jumped up and hit him across the face. At that moment Di came in – her face was white and her eyes red. But she wasted no time.

'Shut up,' she said to Tony, flatly. 'And you shut up too, you soppy little piece,' she remarked to Sandra.

'Brylo, what were you saying? We've got to work fast, the rest are waking and they'll come barging in here . . .'

'You, Di; and me; and Sandra. We'll do what's necessary,' said Brylo.

'I happen to be Captain !' shouted Tony.

But Di turned to him and said, 'Look, Captain Marvel, the whole lot of them are bunging up the corridor already. Get them back into their rooms. Get rid of them. And we'll get rid of – we'll see to the Flight Lieutenant. What do we do, Brylo?'

'There's a big chute with air-locks,' said Brylo.

'When Tony has cleared the corridors, we'll get going. And Sandra can say something . . .'

'Yes,' said Sandra. 'I'll think of something.'

Together, Sandra, Brylo and Di committed the Flight Lieutenant's body to the invisible and boundless void surrounding the ship. Sandra thought hard to remember the words of the burial services; she could remember only the phrase, 'Ashes to ashes, dust to dust.' She thought of the nothingness around them and knew the words were wrong. This was not even a burial, she thought.

In the end, she said, over the blanket-wrapped body resting in the air-lock, these words :

'We know that you meant to help us. We know you meant it for the best. We understand. God will understand. May you find peace with God. God bless you.'

Brylo turned a switch. A door came down so that they

could not see the Flight Lieutenant any more. There was a noise of rushing wind that was cut off by the dull thud of another door closing and a door outside opening. They felt a slight and sudden draught. Brylo kept his hand on the switch. They heard the same sound of opening and closing doors. The door nearest them slid upwards. The space beyond it was empty.

They stood there, looking at the empty space. Sandra said, 'I don't know if I did it right.'

Brylo put a hand on her shoulder and told her, 'You said the right words, Sandra.'

Di said, 'It was all right, what you said, Sandra. I'm sure it was. And don't worry about him any more. It had to happen, and it's over now. I'm glad it's over.'

Sandra thought, I am too. Although he was a grown man, he had been only a boy. Why, if you compared him and Tony, she thought, he was younger than Tony in many ways. She was glad that she had said no more than she had, for all that she had said had been the truth and God wanted to hear only the truth. But had He heard? Suddenly, she had a strong feeling, a certain knowledge, that He had. She knew, quite certainly, that the Flight Lieutenant really would rest in peace and that God really would bless him. She felt as if she had been on trial for her life, and found Not Guilty.

'Let's go and find out what the others are doing,' she said.

Chapter 17

They went back to Control, but no one was there. Brylo discreetly picked up the few things that had belonged to the Flight Lieutenant and put them down a disposal chute.

Then Spadger rushed by in the corridor.

'Where are they all?' shouted Di.

'Meeting in the Captain's cabin!' shouted Spadger, and ran on.

Brylo and Sandra looked at each other wryly. 'We'd better go and see what he's up to now,' said Sandra.

'Captain's cabin! La-di-da!' said Di.

When they got to the big lounge, they found all the children sitting in a circle round Tony, who sat on a raised leather armchair. He was in full spate.

'And there's another thing,' he was saying. 'When you come in here, I don't want you lot making a noise and messing about and sitting in any flippin' chair that takes your fancy – oh, you're here, are you?' he broke off, as Sandra, Brylo and Di came in. 'Di, you can sit on that chair. Brylo, come up here. Sandra, sit with the others.'

'Bossy,' said Di. But Tony had spoken so positively that they obeyed him.

'All right, down to business,' said Tony. 'You probably don't know what's been happening, and I'm going to tell you. The Flight Lieutenant's dead and these three have just come back from burying him. Right? All right. And there's no need for any of you to start talking about it or crying about it or anything else, because it's done and over and that's all there is to it. So *keep quiet*.'

They kept quiet.

'All right, next item,' continued Tony. 'As you all know, we're stuck up here in the middle of nowhere and we've got just as much idea of what to do with ourselves as old Durden has about keeping shop.'

Spadger, Billy and one or two others giggled and Sandra wished they hadn't. She could see trouble coming.

'So I had a think and I thought to myself, "What we've got to do is – do something. It's no good drifting about not knowing where we're going or why or how long. We've got to find out!"'

Tony paused dramatically, then went on.

'And how do you find out? If you'll kindly stop pushing and fidgeting – yes, you, Tiddler! – I'll tell you how you find out. You *ask*. And who do you ask? You ask the people who matter back on Earth. And how do you ask? You ask by radio. Radio! That's the conclusion I came to. Perhaps I was wrong, but that's what I thought. Use your loaf and use the radio, then you'll be ALL RIGHT! OK?'

Sandra's heart sank. He believes every word he's saying, she thought. He's quite forgotten that it was Brylo's idea.

'Of course, on a ship like this, the radio's bound to be a bit complicated. You don't just twiddle a knob on your transistor and get the Beatles. Oh, no! It's not like that at all. Quite frankly, I don't know how to work the radio on this ship. Didn't know then, don't know now. But I knew someone who *did*. . . . No, not you, Brylo boy!'

This got a laugh. Brylo had been staring ahead of himself and biting a thumbnail. He was worried. Tony startled him. Several laughed at his surprise. But Tony wanted more than this.

'The Flight Lieutenant! He's the one, I thought. He'll know about the radio. But he was acting funny. A bit off his rocker. Couldn't get any sense out of him. So I got hold of old Brylo, here, and set him to work on the problem. Brylo's the boy with the brains, I thought . . .' (again, there was some laughter) . . . 'Let *him* fix it. Tell them about it, Brylo !'

Once again, he had Brylo completely off guard. And while Brylo, too surprised to protest, told a limping story about his attempt to make the Flight Lieutenant explain the radio, Tony made faces, picked his nose, crossed and re-crossed his legs and pulled Di's hair. And Sandra thought to herself: 'Why must Tony do this? Why can't he be content?'

Brylo had almost finished his story, when Tony interrupted him.

'Well, thank you for your report, Brylo boy,' said Tony. 'Goes on a bit does our Brylo, but it's all clever stuff. *Brains*, you see !' He twiddled a finger against his forehead and raised a laugh.

'But you didn't tell us one thing, Brylo. You didn't tell us if you got anything out of the Flight Lieutenant with your questions. Did you?'

'You know I didn't,' said Brylo, flustered. 'You know I didn't, because after that, you . . .'

'I took over,' said Tony. 'Yes, I took over. I got to work on the Flight Lieutenant. I thought to myself, if brains won't do it – even Brylo's brains – we'll have to try something a bit different. So I'll tell you what I did. Come a bit closer . . .'

They shuffled forward to make a closer ring and Tony began his story. Sandra watched their faces. Brylo, sullen and humiliated. Di, stroking the leather of the chair she sat on, then stroking her own hair. Beauty, her eyes fixed worshipfully on Tony's face.

The rest of them, completely accepting Tony's leadership.

Then she looked at Tony, telling the story of his triumph with the 'scrambled eggs'. And it had been a triumph, thought Sandra. He had been brilliant to think of it. And Brylo didn't think of it, Tony did. If only, if only, if only, if only Tony would stop puffing himself up and ramming his cleverness down everyone's throat !

Tony came to the end of his story. 'So there it is,' he said, waving a hand in a large gesture. 'You're going to be all right. You're not home and dry yet, mind you – I never said you were – but at least we've got some hope. We've got the radio. We can get in touch with Earth and home. We've got – the – radio !'

They actually applauded ! And Tony, flushed and victorious, could not resist a last jab at Brylo. 'Yes, we've got the radio, thanks to your friend and my friend, Captain Tony. Right, Brylo?'

Several of the children laughed. And Beauty laughed too.

Brylo's dark face did not change expression. He was waiting for that last little jeer, thought Sandra : I wonder what he'll say . . .

'Not quite right, Tony,' said Brylo. 'You've forgotten one thing. We've got the radio, yes. We know how to turn it off and on. We can work it on several frequencies. But we haven't got it on the right frequency, remember?'

Tony's mouth fell open. He *had* forgotten, thought Sandra. He was so pleased with himself that he's forgotten that we never actually got through to anyone.

Tony rose to his feet, trying to take hold of himself.

'Well, for flip's sake ! –' he shouted, furiously, 'I did all the real work – getting the Flight Lieutenant to talk and all that – and all you do is talk about frequencies ! Who cares about flippin' frequencies, the radio's working, isn't it?'

He came towards Brylo – and tripped on the edge of the carpet. Once again, he raised a laugh. But this time, the laugh was against him. And Beauty, quite innocently, laughed too.

'Funny Tony !' she said, delightedly.

Tony turned and hit her across the face, hard.

There was complete silence. Beauty fell on her side, then propped herself up again on one plump little hand. The other explored her face. There was a vivid red print of Tony's fingers on it. Big tears filled her eyes and ran down her cheeks. At last, she gave a wail and began to cry.

Sandra ran to her and put her arms round her. The rest stood up, uneasily. But their eyes never left Tony's face.

Billy Bason moved towards Tony and stood in front of him, staring hard at him. He pulled Tiddler forward in front of Tony, and said, mildly, 'Here, Tony – sorry, *Captain* Tony – why don't you have a smash at the Tiddler? He's nice and small, too.'

'That's right, Captain, have a bash at Tiddler . . .'

'You like 'em small don't you, Captain?'

'Go on, Tony, you're much bigger than him. Hit him !'

'I'll smash the lot of you, see if I don't !' muttered Tony, scarlet-faced.

'He could, too !' said Di coming to Tony's side. Her eyes were blazing.

Tony had not moved. But now, he flung off Di's hand and walked to his big leather chair. He sat down in it slowly, folded his arms, and stared straight ahead.

'I'm still Captain !' he said. 'You lot get out. Get out of my cabin ! GET OUT !'

Without looking at him, they left.

Only Di remained with Tony.

She remained sitting in the same big armchair and continued to stroke the leather with her finger. She noticed that her nails were growing to a nice shape. She wondered how much longer they would grow before they got back to Earth.

'You stupid fool,' she said. Tony did not answer.

'What did you want to go and hit her for?' she said. 'They'll hate you for that . . .'

'That's right, now *you* start,' said Tony.

'It was all right before. You'd got what you wanted. You got this room, and you were the Captain.'

'I hadn't got the radio, but I'm still the Captain,' said Tony. 'Remember that.'

Di got up from her armchair and walked over to Tony. She put her hand on his forearm and said, quietly, 'Tony, what's the matter with you? Just when you'd done something really clever, just when you'd got them all on your side, you have to go and ruin it all. Showing off ! Then hitting Beauty ! And before that, they were eating out of your hand . . .'

'They hate me,' said Tony. 'Everyone hates me. They always have . . .'

Di could think of nothing to say.

'*I'll show them,*' said Tony. He spoke in a low, ferocious voice. The sound of it frightened Di. What does it matter, she thought, whether they hate you or not? I know what they think of me, back at Little Mowlesbury. But what did it matter? She wouldn't stay there a minute longer than she needed. When she was fifteen or sixteen, she'd shake the dust of the place off her feet. She'd go to London. She'd be part of the swinging scene !

'Little Mowlesbury !' she sneered. 'What's it matter what Little Mowlesbury thinks. Dead square . . .'

'I'll show them,' said Tony, venomously.

Di shrugged and pressed a button for an egg salad. Nothing happened.

'Press it again,' said Tony.

She did, but no egg salad came out. Tony strode over and jabbed the button again and again. It was useless. He swore, kicked at a chair, and shouted to Di, 'Well at least there's plenty of wine left !' And he strode out to get a bottle.

Chapter 18

No one noticed that one person had been absent from the meeting in the Captain's cabin. That person was Ashley.

He lay in his seat among the radio-communication apparatus. The shelves above his head were filled with neat lines of
plates each filled with an egg salad. He had crept out and
stolen them from the Captain's cabin, brought them back
two at a time, and arranged the salads so that each egg was on
the left of its plate. It was tidier that way, and Mummy loved
tidiness.

The earphones were still on the floor, whistling faintly but
shrilly. He had forgotten his fear of them. He picked them
up and turned them over in his hands idly. Then he put
them on his chest, reached up and turned the first knob his
fingers touched. The whistling warbled and fluctuated, then
stopped.

This interested him slightly – enough to make him stand
up and put the earphones on. He arranged them so that they
did not cover his ears: he did not want that nasty screaming
in his ears again. 'Never put things in your ears,' Mummy
had told him.

He extended a hand to the knobs and dials. One of his
finger-nails had a black rim of dirt. He said, 'Tch! Tch!
Dirty!' and looked for his comb. He broke off one of the teeth
and cleaned the dirty fingernail. But perhaps he should not
have broken the comb, he told himself. It looked untidy with
a tooth missing. What would Mummy say?

He thought about this for some time, then tried to put the
tooth back in the comb. It went into position perfectly, but

then fell on the floor. Mummy used to tell him a story about a lady who was going to be married; the lady was untidy and had let a pin fall on the floor and not bothered to pick it up. On her wedding day, she had needed a pin dreadfully badly, because her wedding dress was torn. The guests were all at the church, the organ was playing, the bridegroom was standing ready at the altar – but where was the bride? (Mummy used to make her eyes round and hold her hands up when she came to this part of the story.) Why, the bride was on her hands and knees, still looking for the pin! And in the end, because of her untidiness, the lady never did get to the church to get married. All because she had left a pin on the floor.

Ashley bent down to pick up the tooth from the comb. Ah, there it was, near the corner! He supported himself with his left hand and reached for the tooth with the right. His left hand slipped slightly and brushed over a number of keys and switches on the radio console. And suddenly! –

'WELL, LATEBIRDS,' said the earphones, loud and clear, 'SEEMS THAT A LOT OF YOU HAVE BEEN DIGGING THAT FAST-RISING GROUP, THE LITTLE DARLINS! AND CONFIDENTIALLY, FOLKS, YOURS TRULY KINDA DIGS THEM TOO! SO LET'S DIG THAT LITTLE BIT DEEPER, SHALL US? – RIGHT BACK INTO THE ROOTS OF A GROUP THAT COULD BE MAKING POP HISTORY . . . RIGHT BACK TO ONE OF THEIR FIRST RELEASES . . .'

Ashley stared unseeingly ahead of himself, holding the tooth of the comb in his fingers.

'. . . ONE THAT NEVER MADE THE CHARTS, BUT IT'S A VERY SWINGING, VERY PRETTY LITTLE DITTY FOR ALL THAT. SEE IF YOU AGREE AS THE LITTLE DARLINS PLAY IT SWEET AND TENDER WITH . . . "DOLLY MOMMA"!'

Ashley did not move. He stared unblinkingly ahead.

'DOLLY MOMMA . . .' sang the four voices, lovingly, 'YOU'RE SO LITTLE AND CUTE . . . IN MY HEART . . . YOU HAVE JUST TAKEN ROOT . . . IN MY DREAMS . . . YOU'LL

ALWAYS BE THERE ... I KNEW JUST WHERE ... I
COULD FIND YOU MY DEAR ...'

Ashley did not move.

'BUT YOU'VE CH-AY-AY-AY-ANGED!' howled the singers.
'WHY DID YOU GO AWAY, DOLLY MOMMA! ... WHEN
I BEGGED YOU TO STAY ... IN MY ARMS! ... WHERE
YOU BELONG! ... IT'S SO WRONG! ... YOU NEVER
SHOULD GO! ... I'VE BEEN MISSING YOU SO!'
A female voice of piercing sweetness took over the melody.
Ashley did not move.

'I'LL RETURN ...' promised the voice, in a catchy, flutter-
ing soprano, 'I'LL BE DRYING EACH TEAR ... HELD SO
TIGHT! ... HOLD ME CLOSER, MY DEAR! ... ETERN-
ALLY ... MINE'S THE VOICE THAT YOU'LL HEAR —
YOUR DOLLY MOMMA ...'

'DOLLY MOMMA ...' echoed the Little Darlins.

'DOLLY MOMMA ...'

'DOLLY MOMMA ...'

Ashley took the earphones from his head and blinked his
eyes. He seemed to be considering. He flung the earphones
with all his strength into the corner. The jack-plug jerked
from the console as they disconnected. Ashley's lower lip
trembled.

'I want my Mummy,' he said. 'You're not my Mummy.'

Brylo walked away from the meeting in the Captain's cabin almost blind with anger. He could feel his own fury pounding in the sides of his head; could feel a headache tightening a red band round his brow.

He strode down the corridor and blundered into Sandra, who was carrying a tear-stained Beauty in her arms.

'Oh, Brylo!' began Sandra, 'Wasn't it awful, hitting Beauty. . . .' But Brylo went on, hardly hearing.

'Brylo is cruel too!' cried Beauty after him, and more tears came.

'Wrong again!' said Brylo to himself. 'Wrong again! Idiot! Why didn't you say something to Beauty? Why didn't you make her smile, make her like you? Why didn't you capture her now that she hates her old hero, Tony? Why didn't you say something to Sandra? Why don't you get Beauty and Sandra and all the rest of them to follow *you*, to make you their leader?'

He reached his cabin, shut the door and flung himself down. Think! he told himself. It never seems to get you anywhere, but think! Pretend you are writing it all down on a sheet of paper . . .

Why do you want to be the leader?
Because very soon there must be a leader – a real leader. Not Tony.

Why not Tony? Because you envy him? Because you're half afraid of him?

No, because we cannot go on like this. I do often envy Tony and I am afraid of him.

Why?

Because he can always . . . get at me. Through my colour.

But that isn't all. If I were the same colour as he, it would make no difference. He would still find some weakness and make use of it – he would still think and act faster than me. He would do something flashier, 'cleverer' . . . Like his trick with the 'scrambled eggs'.

So why should you be the leader?

Ah, thought Brylo, stirring on his bed. That is the real question. Answer that one! He lay back and imagined the sheet of paper again . . .

Why? Because so far we have just been a lot of silly kids stuck in space. But now, things must change.

Either they will get slowly worse or violently different.

Take 'slowly worse' first . . .

Well, suppose that we do *not* manage to get in touch with Earth. Suppose that we are entirely forgotten and adrift in space for ever. Suppose that we run out of food and air and water . . . Someone must take charge. It will be awful, but someone must do it.

But why?

Because it would not be . . . dignified . . . to come to the end and die in Tony's way. Everything would be in a mess . . .

But how would your leadership make it better? Never mind . . . What if things become 'violently different'?

It's obvious: everything will be different once we get in touch with Earth. Then, we will not be just a lot of bodies, adrift in space; we will have things to learn, things to do, to help ourselves get back to Earth. And the sorts of things that we will have to learn and do are the sorts of things that I can do and Tony cannot.

Why?

Because they will be technical things. Understanding instructions, for example. Learning to use all the instruments in Control. Learning to navigate and direct the ship. Tony could never learn things of that kind. I could.

But you are not yet in touch with Earth. The radio is not yet working.

No.

Then why are you lying in bed?

Brylo jerked himself out of bed, washed his face with cold water, picked up the notes marked 'Radio', and made purposefully for Control. He did not even notice that his headache was gone.

Chapter 20

Control was deserted. Brylo snapped on the lights and went to work. With the help of his notes, he repeated the whole sequence of operations that he had watched the Flight Lieutenant carry out. As he worked, he made more notes. So much of what the Flight Lieutenant had done was unnecessary, or repetitive, or even meaningless.

A steady hum grew in the loudspeakers. Brylo paused. 'Recap,' he muttered. He began to realize that despite its seeming complexity, this was a fairly ordinary radio. It's a pity, he thought, that radio is not really my subject. . . . But on the other hand, it is obvious that I do not have to understand radio to work it. After all, there's nothing wrong with this equipment. It's only the missing frequency band that I must sort out . . .

He worked on. The hum remained constant. The excitement that had possessed him at the beginning began to wear off : worry took its place. Why, he wondered, am I getting *nothing*? Why aren't any stations coming through – even if they are the wrong ones? Then suddenly he noticed that he had failed to readjust a 'Gain' knob that he had turned down – he had not wanted to produce any of the howls and shrieks that had happened before. He turned the knob.

'SO LET'S DIG THAT LITTLE BIT DEEPER, SHALL US?' said the loudspeaker. 'RIGHT BACK INTO THE ROOTS OF A GROUP THAT COULD BE MAKING POP HISTORY –'

Brylo's heart leapt ! So did his hands. He lowered the volume. At all costs, he wanted to avoid interruption. Particularly from Tony.

The voice from the loudspeaker burbled on, quietly now. 'See if you agree, as the Little Darlins play it sweet and tender with ... Dolly Momma !' it said. The sugar-sweet smile in the voice was vaguely familiar to Brylo. He knew he had heard it before. Where? That's right – at home ! It was one of those continental stations that put out pop most of the night and day. Which means, thought Brylo, that I am on the right frequency after all !

He was about to explore the tuning dials to see what other stations he could get, when caution stopped him. First, he thought, I will note the position of all the dials. It would be terrible to lose this station and not be able to find it again ...

He began jotting down notes. Now the group was singing. Something about Dolly Momma going away, and missing her so, and holding you tight. The usual nonsense. Yet to me, thought Brylo, it's the most wonderful and exciting song I will ever hear. It means that Earth remains : that there hasn't been a war, that people are still doing the same things they always did.... It means that we might possibly get home – and that there is a home to go to.

They were coming to the end of the song. Brylo put down his ballpoint to listen. I must remember this, he thought – must remember the very words they sing. 'Dolly Momma ! ...' crooned the singers. 'Dolly Momma ... Dolly Momma ! ...' It was the end of the song.

But Brylo still waited, his head cocked and his ballpoint idle. What would they play next? And would there be a station identification? He waited – and actually heard the announcer draw breath to speak as the station went dead ! All that was left was the slight 'live' hum of the loudspeaker.

Brylo felt a sick wave of panic : he checked it. Don't touch anything, he told himself. Just *think* ...

But all he could think of was the terrible loss. That had been Earth – and now it was gone. It had been the promise of home – and now the promise was broken.

'Think !' he said, out loud.

A fault in the radio? If that was the trouble, then things were really serious. He would be able neither to find the fault nor correct it. Best to assume that it was something else ...

He buried his head in his hands and tried to think. A voice very close to him said, 'Don't want to fall asleep on the job, Brylo boy!'

It was Tony.

When Brylo, unwillingly, had explained what had happened, it was Tony who guessed the answer.

'Seen anything of dear little Ashley?' Tony said musingly. 'I haven't. Wasn't at my meeting, come to think of it. And he lives in his cosy little nest in ...'

'The Communications room!' Brylo finished for him. 'That could be it! It's just possible that Ashley is the one who ...'

'Let's get going,' said Tony tightly, and led Brylo down the corridor to Communications. As they reached it, they heard the soft click of a lock.

Tony seized the knob on the door and twisted it. It would not open. He shook it and rattled it and tore at it. He was about to shout something when Brylo silenced him with a look and whispered, 'Don't frighten him! Quietly!'

'Ashley!' said Tony, in a reasonable voice. 'This is Captain Tony. Be a good boy and open the door!'

Silence.

'I'll try!' muttered Brylo. 'Come on, Ashley!' he said, 'you want to go home, don't you? You want to see your Mummy? Well, if you open this door, we can all get home! Come on, Ashley ... open it!'

Silence.

'That's right, Ashley, your mummy's waiting!' said Tony, hoarsely. 'You want to see your mummy, don't you?'

They heard Ashley move inside the Communications room! And then his babyish voice, on the edge of tears, shouted, 'I won't! I won't! That lady on the wireless – she wasn't my mummy!'

Tony, Brylo, Di and Sandra held a council of war in Control.

'Look, if you woke me up and got me in here simply to help you drive the poor little thing mad ...' Sandra was saying.

'We flippin' got to get in there,' said Tony savagely.

'Not by breaking down the door! Can't you see, he's hysterical already! He's going all ... peculiar! And if you break down the door, you'll finish him! He'll go really hysterical! And we just won't be able to cope, not with all the others as well ...'

'If you break down the door,' Di said, 'the others will come tearing down the corridor to see what the noise is. They're asleep at the moment. But if you get the whole mob down here ...'

'I need a flippin' drink ...' said Tony, gloomily. Di rounded on him.

'That's just what you don't need, Master Captain Tony!' she stormed. 'You're Captain, remember that, and this is serious, so you can jolly well behave properly just this once and not make an exhibition of yourself.'

They were staggered by her outburst. They were almost as much surprised by Tony's response.

'All right, keep your hair on,' he said, mildly.

There was an awkward pause. Then Sandra jumped up and said, 'Tony's right, we do need a drink! I'll go and make something ...'

She ran out. The rest sat in Control, exhausted. Sandra, in the kitchen, thought, 'Tea? Can't be bothered. Coffee? Just as much trouble as tea.' She cast her eye over the tins and jars. 'Oh, well,' she said, 'even if we're never, ever, going to get any sleep, we might as well have a night-cap ...'

And she made four cups of hot Ovaltine.

She put the steaming cups on the tray and walked up the corridor, treading softly. She noticed as she passed it that there was a very slight sound from behind the door of the Communications room. In Control, she handed round the cups. The smell was delicious.

'This flippin' muck,' said Tony, dismally. But he drank his with the rest.

'We've got to find a way,' continued Tony, sipping his Ovaltine. 'Can't we think of some bait, some reward, to...'

Di held up a warning hand and pursed her lips to imitate the sound 'Shh!' For standing at the door, rubbing his sleepy eyes with the back of his hand, was Ashley!

'Mummy's here!' he said. 'She's bringing my drinkie! I can smell it!'

'That's all right, love,' said Sandra, managing to keep her voice even. 'Come over here and share mine!'

Ten minutes later, Ashley was happily asleep in bed, tucked in by Sandra; and coming through the loudspeakers in Control was the sound of the Home Service from London.

'. . . and now, the news,' said the BBC voice.

Sandra and Di reached for each other's hands and held tight. Brylo and Tony exchanged a glance.

'The Pian Tuk talks, now in their third day, will shortly end. Although no official announcements will be made until the conclusion of the talks, Mr Tang, at a news conference, expressed himself as more than satisfied with the western powers' proposals. And when our spokesman at the talks, Mr Trueman, left the conference chamber at the end of to-day's session, he was seen to be . . .' here the announcer made his voice respectably winsome . . . 'smiling broadly. Tomor-row, the agenda will include the disputed issue of the . . .'

'I don't like this programme,' said Ashley, petulantly.

'Drink your flippin' drink,' said Tony, quietly and venom-ously. Ashley shut up.

The news continued. It spoke of rain stopping play, of sterling balances, of disagreement over the proposals for the Channel Tunnel.

'Same old guff,' commented Tony. 'What price the Flight Lieutenant now? Stupid nit. . . .'

'The children in space,' said the announcer. The children tensed. 'Today, the third day, renewed efforts were made to establish communication with the missing space craft; but again, without success. The automatic sender on the craft indicates that it is moving steadily away from Earth towards the sun. In reply to a question in the House of Commons, the Minister of Defence said that despite protracted consultation with scientists of seven countries, including Russia and Amer-ica, no suggestions had been forthcoming as to possible in-terception of the children's craft by another. The craft was by now well outside the limits reached by any space craft, manned or unmanned, sent from Earth. Messages of sympathy and condolence have been pouring into Little Mowlesbury, home of the missing children, from all corners of the globe. At Downing Street, the parents of the children were received by . . .'

'Can I go to bed now?' said Ashley. Once again, he was viciously silenced by Tony. They missed several sentences.

'The Minister of Defence reiterated that there was no reason to suppose that the children are not alive. The craft was generously provisioned with ample supplies of air, food and water. The Minister once again declined to comment on the rôle of Flight Lieutenant Barclay. He merely repeated that the flight was unauthorized. Asked for further details of the space craft, the Minister refused to reply, saying that it was not in the public interest to release any information at the present time.'

They heard the announcer shuffle his papers. Then – 'By international agreement a continuous radio signal consisting of the word Earth in morse is being beamed at the craft on the following frequencies: 15.9, 200 and 1300 metres. I will repeat those frequencies: 15.9, 200, 1300. The signal is continuous except for transmissions in spoken words every hour on the hour . . .'

Four heads turned to the clock on the wall. They had forty-three minutes before the next spoken transmission . . .

Brylo went to work. 'I'm going to try and pick up the steady transmission – the morse transmission,' he said, 'What's "Earth" in morse code? . . .'

His hands shook as he wrote:

                    E .
                    A . _
                    R . _ .
                    T _
                    H . . . .

'Dit, dit da, dit da dit, da, dit dit dit dit . . .' he repeated to himself – and almost flung himself at the radio console.

'Dead,' he muttered to himself, then rushed from the room into Ashley's cabin. They followed him and lived with him through the agonizing pauses when he clutched his hair with one hand and his notes with the other – then sprang to his feet to try another combination of setting on the Communications Room radio console. For once, Tony was completely silent. He spoke no word, made no unnecessary movement, showed not a trace of expression.

'All right, that should be it,' mumbled Brylo. 'We should be able to hear it in here on the monitor – no, let's go back to Control, where the big speakers are . . .'

They trooped back. The clock said three minutes to the hour. 'Nicely timed,' said Tony – the first words he had spoken.

Brylo's brown hands scrabbled over the controls of the radio console. There was a brief shriek from the loudspeakers which Brylo cut with a flick of a dial – then, to a fluctuating background of howls and flutings and whistles, the sound they had been waiting for. *Da. Dit da. Dit da dit. Da. Dit dit dit dit.*

They cheered, but Brylo stopped them by pointing to the clock. One and a half minutes to go . . .

The second hand silently and greasily slid its way round the slickly-styled clock face. Brylo caught himself wondering why the hands did not show fractions of sections, then remembered the array of 'precision' time pieces and stopwatches built into what looked like a navigation console nearby. Thank heavens, he thought, that we may soon be finished with loose time, endless time, time on our hands. Soon we may be talking in split seconds, milliseconds – the precisely calculated fragments of time and distance that will mark our journey home . . .

At that moment, the morse code cut out : a different sound filled the loudspeakers : and a voice spoke !

Chapter 22

'This is Earth calling !' began the voice. 'This is Earth calling the children in the space craft, the children from Little Mowlesbury. And Flight Lieutenant Barclay. This is Earth calling you . . .'

The voice fell on them like a soft blow. It was a surprising voice – kindly, informal, a little tired, dutiful, matter-of-fact. But most of all, it was a voice that seemed amazingly close at hand. None of the children would have been surprised if its owner had walked in at the door. And each would have expected to see much the same man – a man in late middle age, probably in uniform, with a disciplined but pleasant face. The sort of man that, if you fell off your bike and gave yourself a really nasty knock, would pick you up and dust you down and see you home. Without fuss.

'He seems so near . . .' said Sandra. 'I'll get the others !' She ran out. And later, as the voice continued speaking, there came a ring of faces at the door of Control, all intently listening.

'This is another of the regular hourly broadcasts,' said the voice. 'I wonder if you've heard any of them? Of course, we quite understand that you may have heard all of them, but cannot reply. That is why, at the end of this broadcast, in five minutes time, I am going to repeat exact instructions for using all the communications apparatus on board your craft – the radio. But first, messages from home – incidentally, the whole world has been sending you messages . . . we had a post of four thousand letters today, including several from Pian Tuk, where the peace talks are going on. And going well. In fact, the President wrote . . .'

'So the Flight Lieutenant wasn't so mad after all!' whispered Sandra to Brylo, as the voice read the message.

'But you'll be wanting to hear from your parents,' continued the voice. 'Let's start with the youngest. Here's a message for you, Beauty! Your mother says she loves you very much and she knows you're being a good girl because you always are, and are you saying your prayers every night? Ask Sandra to help you with them if you forget them. And your dad sends you a big kiss and says he'll soon have you sitting on his lap again . . .'

Sandra saw Beauty's face, smiling uncertainly when her name was first mentioned, then beaming as the voice spoke of sitting on her dad's lap. 'I did say my prayers . . .' said Beauty loudly. 'Tell Mummy!'

The voice went on. There were messages for each of the children and also for the Flight Lieutenant. As each message came through, a face within Control room would become fixed in concentration. At the end, a head would be lifted and there would be a slow and private smile.

'He's all right, that bloke,' said Tony, nonchalantly. But you could see that he too was strongly stirred by the voice from home.

'That's the end of the messages,' said the voice. 'I will repeat them – and perhaps some new ones – in an hour's time. Now I am going to break off for seven seconds to repeat the call sign, EARTH, in morse code. Listen to it. Tune to it . . .'

They heard the already familiar pattern of the morse code. Then, the voice repeated the frequencies they should tune to, and said good night.

Immediately, another voice took over. 'Communications,' it stated baldly. 'This is what you do to get in touch with Earth by radio. Write down what I am going to tell you. This is what you do. This is how you operate your radio. Listen and write it down. Are you ready? Write it down . . .'

'Must think we're barmy !' said Tony – then suddenly realized that this was just what the people on Earth might be taking into account. How could they know what was going on in the space craft?

'Sit in the seat facing the radio console in Control,' began the voice (Brylo was already sitting there). 'You will recognize this console by . . .'

Brylo listened. The rest were whispering to each other. Brylo wrote. Tony stared ahead, seeing nothing. Was he listening too?

The voice, cold and clear, went on. Brylo stretched out a hand now and then to touch a control the voice had mentioned, then wrote again. The children's whispering grew into a babble.

'Shut up,' said Tony. The babble died.

'I will now recap,' said the voice. 'First, ensure that each control facing you is set as I have told you. Then take the instructions you have written down at my dictation to the communications room and set the console there according to those instructions. You are then free to send – free to transmit in plain speech through the microphone – to Earth. Remember the four seconds interval between sending and receiving. Remember to say "over" when you have finished speaking. Transmit at any time. Do it soon. Do it *now*.'

Brylo swept his hands over a row of switches. The loudspeakers were instantly silent. So were the children. He swung round in the swivel chair to face them. Everything was utterly still and silent.

'All right, then?' said Tony, hoarsely.

'Yes. We can send.'

'Let's get weaving,' said Tony.

'Calling Earth !' said Brylo. He cleared his throat and said it again, this time clearly. 'Calling *Earth* !'

'Say "Over" !' hissed Tony.

'Calling Earth ! Over !' said Brylo.

'Flick the flippin' *switch* !' said Tony. Brylo started, then flicked a tiny switch on the hand microphone. The loud-speaker filled the room with sound – with a cosmic litter of echoing trills that sounded like laughter, with the hiss and sputter of frying food, with a hollow, endless note like the dying call of an operatic soprano.

'They're not . . .' began Tony.

'Wait – time lag !' replied Brylo, urgently.

Then they heard it – a voice that distinctly said, 'My God ! It's them !. . . Come in, space craft ! Come in !' said the voice, recovering itself. 'Come in ! Keep talking ! Over !'

'It's *us* . . .' began Brylo weakly. Tony leaned over and with furious impatience, clicked the switch on the microphone. 'Now *speak* !' he shouted.

'Hallo, Earth, this is the space ship – the one from Little Mowlesbury. It's *us* ! Over !'

Another four seconds of silence. Then : 'I hear you, I hear you !' cried the voice. 'Reception fair ! Your signal coming through OK ! OK ! Keep talking ! Over !'

Brylo's face was working. Tony snatched the microphone handset from him and almost spat words into the microphone.

'Hallo Earth, it's the Little Mowlesbury space ship ! This is Tony Hoskings, Captain Tony Hoskings, I'm running this ship and we're all all right ! All all right except the Flight Lieutenant, he's dead ! All the children well, got that? – all well. Did you get that? Over !'

Again the pause, and then : 'Message received and under-stood, you are all well, Flight Lieutenant dead. Have you dis-posed of body?' Again, they caught an aside : 'Poor little devils !' the voice said. 'Have you disposed of body? Over !'

'Yes, through the big air-lock, but never mind that, what do we do to get back to Earth? *Can we get back to Earth?*'

They listened through the never-ending four-second pause. Then the voice from Earth spoke again.

'We'll get you back. Somehow. We'll get you back. But

you will have a lot to learn and you will have to learn fast. We will start immediately. Which one of you is best at school? Which one is best at mathematics – the best at school subjects? Is it you, Tony? Over.'

During the next four seconds they watched Tony's face and saw written on it the fight that was going on inside him. They watched as he pressed the button on the handset and saw his lips twist as he spoke.

'Hallo, Earth. You want brains, you want Brylo. He's the clever boy. I'm only the Captain. Here you are, Brylo boy . . .'

He handed over the microphone and walked out of Control without a glance at any of them.

Chapter 23

But very soon, Tony came back. By then Brylo had already covered several sheets of paper. He seldom spoke unless to say, 'Yes, receiving you. Over.' Tony quietly cleared the rest of the children from the room and made them go to their beds. Then he looked closely at Brylo's face. The brown skin was pasty, the eyes red-rimmed. He took the handset from Brylo and spoke.

'This is Captain Tony Hoskings speaking. He's had enough, Brylo has – the one you've been speaking to. He's gone a long time without sleep. We all of us have. He ought to rest. What say? Over.'

The pause, then: 'All right, let him rest. He's done well, he's very quick. Make him go to bed. You hear that, Brylo? Go to bed, you've done a good job so far. Tell you what – leave the set on, we'll give you an alarm call in three hours. We'll clear the air now, and alert you in three hours. Understood? Over.'

'Wait a minute!' said Tony, after the pause. 'He'll need longer than that – he's flaked out, I tell you! Can't you give him six hours? Over.'

The pause. Then 'Six hours? Not a chance. We've got to act fast and so have you. Didn't you know? You're heading for the sun!'

Tony gasped and turned white. 'We'll be fried!' he said to Brylo.

'No, it's not as bad as that,' Brylo replied. 'It's a long way to the sun. A very long way. What they're worried about is communications. The further away we get, the nearer we get to the sun, the worse radio contact gets. They're worried about interference – about our radio reception. It isn't all that good some of the time – an awful lot of background noise, great waves of it. It gets tiring.... And it could get worse.'

'Three hours, then,' said Tony into the microphone. 'Brylo's going to bed now – off you go, Brylo – and I'll stand by here in case there's anything you want to tell me. Good night. Over.'

'Good night. God bless you all. Over,' replied the voice from Earth. The loudspeakers suddenly became silent but for the morse. *Dit, dit da, dit da dit, da, dit dit dit dit* it went, endlessly.

Tony didn't even notice. Pausing only to make sure that he was alone, he closed the door to Control, sat down in the seat that Brylo had left, clutched his temples in either hand and began to read Brylo's notes.

As he read, his eyes darted from the papers to the controls they described. Sometimes he got up and looked carefully at a particular control set-up. As he looked, his lips moved, repeating the words he had read. Sometimes, his concentration was broken by a fit of impatience or despair. He would mutter in puzzlement or disgust. But he worked steadily on as the minutes and the hours passed unnoticed.

Just before the loudspeaker came to life again and the voice from Earth called for Brylo, Tony thrust the papers away from him and muttered the words he had spoken earlier.

'*I'll show them!*' he said.

Chapter 24

Four hours later.

'All right, we've got to try it some time. Let's try it now!' said the voice from Earth. 'All right Brylo? Over.'

'All right,' said Brylo dully. 'Over. No, come back – let's get it right. I'm to operate directional drives only, check? Over.'

'Directional drives only, check. In other words, Brylo, you're going to give the ship a mild nudge employing ONLY the main drive motors you're using now to stabilize your flight. No atomic drive, no rockets. So don't sound so worried, it's not much different from turning up the gas! Anyhow, it isn't the motors we're interested in: what we want you to do is to check the change in course from the instruments once you've *used* the drive deflection. All right, let's do it! Over!'

Brylo, closely watched by Tony, left his chair and walked over to another console. He hesitated, then took hold of two hammer-shaped levers by their heads.

'Am about to operate Left 1 and Left 2, now both at ...' he quickly checked the position of the levers' shafts on the graduated scales ... '0.5. Am now moving them to 0.6 ... 0.7 ... 0.8. Left 1 and Left 2 at 0.8! Over.'

'Big deal,' muttered Tony, during the pause.

'Well done, Brylo!' said the voice from Earth. 'You got the drill right! Always get the drill right! Always report to us like that, it matters more than anything else! Now ... do you feel any difference in the ship? Over.'

'Nothing to report. No change. Over.'

'Fine. As I told you, what you've done is to very gently nudge the ship to port – to the left. In another few hours, you'll have changed course a bit and that's all to the good. Sure there are no changes? No difference in the note from the ship for instance? Over.'

'Nothing to report. Over.'

'All right, now give me a series of course readings taken at ten second intervals. Can you manage them that fast? Over.'

'I could manage them faster than that – never mind, I'll stick to ten seconds. Stand by, do not contact me until you have received six readings. Over!'

Brylo swivelled in his chair with a movement that was soon to become second nature to him, and fastened his eyes on a display with three crossed pointers. Simultaneously he adjusted a switch on a clock which zeroed itself and began to tick off seconds.

'Brainy Brylo!' Tony whispered to himself. But he watched every move.

'Oh four, seven oh,' said Brylo. 'Oh four, seven one ... Oh four, seven one ... Oh four, seven two ...' Tony stood by his shoulder watching the hairline hand of the clock. He felt a savage thrust of impatience, but held it back.

'Oh four, seven four. That is all. Over.' He waited.

'That flippin' pause,' said Tony, and endured it. Then the Earth voice spoke.

'Excellent, Brylo! You're a bright lad! We were afraid the nonsequential co-ordinates might throw you. You see the whole thing is based on a progression of – well, never mind, you're doing fine. Rest for five minutes, you've earned it! For five minutes, over and out.'

The loudspeaker hushed. Brylo sat back in the chair and whistled his breath out. He smiled slightly with relief, then turned to Tony and said, 'Wow! ... Do you think you could get me something to drink, Tony?'

'*Captain* Tony!' shouted Tony.

But he stumped out and came back within the five minutes with hot cocoa.

Chapter 25

It went on for two days. They were days in which Brylo learned and listened and made notes and calculations and trial runs and performed simulated operations as dress rehearsals for the real thing: days in which Tony sulked and muttered and exploded in sudden furies – but watched and listened constantly.

'What's it all in aid of?' Tony demanded during a rest period on the second day. 'What's it flippin' *for*?'

'It's to teach me to operate the ship,' said Brylo, his voice high with exasperation and tiredness. 'You know that as well as I do! It's to teach us how to get home...'

'What do you mean, home? Why was that bloke raving on about the Moon Station? What's that got to do with home?'

Earlier, the voice from Earth had told Brylo that no one yet knew where the ship was to be landed. Some experts wanted a desert landing, some a sea landing – and some, a landing on the moon. Tony had missed the real point of the arguments. Brylo had not...

'The Moon Station? Well, they've got to land us somewhere,' said Brylo, 'And the moon has a nice soft surface and a whole lot of specialized, concentrated equipment all ready to deal with us. After that, they'd ferry us to Earth...'

'In a pig's eye!' said Tony. 'We're landing on Earth if I have anything to do with it!'

'But Tony,' said Brylo, rubbing his tired eyes. 'You haven't anything to do with it. So shut up.' He stopped rubbing his eyes and stared hard and unblinkingly at Tony.

Tony felt something swell in his head and threaten to burst. He felt himself choke with fury. Yet he held back.

'Brylo the Brains,' he said softly. 'Not Brylo the Brawn. Talking flippin' tough, aren't you, Brylo? Proper Cassius Clay. Big mouth and all!'

'And all?' said Brylo. 'Go on . . .'

'Why can't we land on Earth?' yelled Tony.

'Go on about me and Cassius Clay,' said Brylo. 'Me and Cassius Clay – and all?'

'WHY NOT EARTH?' screamed Tony.

'Shut up, and I'll tell you!' shouted Brylo. All right, he thought, I'll leave the Cassius Clay thing until later. But later, I'll . . .

'All right, tell me,' said Tony, very mildly. And he thought, that one got home. That's the thing old Brylo boy can't stand. I'll stick the old needle in his brown skin again later . . .

'All right, *Captain* Tony, try and get your thick head to understand this!' began Brylo, forcing himself to keep his voice low. 'This ship is a sort of bomb. An atomic bomb. The radiation from the nuclear motor killed the Flight Lieutenant, you remember? So it's a sort of bomb that doesn't even have to go off to kill people. Now, if it did go off, it could wipe out half England for all I know. . . .'

'For all you know!' jeered Tony. But he listened.

'My guess is,' continued Brylo, taking no notice of Tony, 'that they're terrified of us on Earth. Terrified of us landing! Think of it from their point of view. The only people they've talked to – the only people they can talk to – are a couple of schoolkids. You and me. One of the schoolkids is being made to learn how to fly a space ship. I've got to learn it in days and learn it by radio. No blackboard, even . . .'

'I thought we'd got telly,' said Tony, shaken.

'What you call "telly" is just an old lady's reading glasses. This ship's telly is just its eyes. And they're short-sighted. They can only see the empty space around us. Nothing to do with Earth telly. Get it?'

'All right, I only thought...'

'As I was saying, they're terrified of us landing on Earth. If I get the landing wrong – BARRROOM! Even a sea landing doesn't cut out the risk very much. And if we made a good landing, this ship might sink. But that's another story. The real thing – or this is what I guess – they want us to land near the Moon Station because it's got a good surface, because it's got every sort of gadget to help us and them... and most important of all, because if the whole thing blows up, it will only black the eye of the Man in the Moon instead of wiping out London or New York or something... And I'll tell you what else I think. I think they're quite right, and I think that you're mad to make such a fuss about it. You'll end up at home either way – IF we get home at all. So what does it matter to you, Earth or Moon, what's the difference?'

'Yeah, what's it matter?' said Tony, quietly. 'What's the difference, eh, Brylo?' He walked away and began to whistle, repetitively and annoyingly. He seemed entirely to have forgotten the argument.

Brylo felt the old, familiar feeling of useless, churning resentment – the feeling of defeat in a battle that did not matter and had no meaning yet was somehow important. He turned on the ship's TV. 'Look, Tony,' he said, as the screen became luminous. Tony came over to look but did not stop whistling.

They stood side by side as the screen filled with a black glow of nothingness. Once, a tiny particle of light shot across the blackness. 'Shooting star,' said Tony.

'No, just the TV tube,' said Brylo. 'There's nothing there to see. Nothing.'

'Turn it through 360 degrees,' said Tony. Brylo, mildly surprised that Tony used the phrase '360 degrees' for 'full circle' – and equally surprised to find that Tony had picked up something of the working of the TV – operated a knob like a gear lever. 'It swings the viewing system,' he began.

'Yes, I know,' said Tony. 'Angle of acceptance, forty-five

degrees. Push this knob here and you get it sort of telephoto. Zoom lens sort of thing. I'm not dim, you know . . .'

No, you're not, thought Brylo. When was it, he thought, that Earth and I talked about this TV set-up? Yesterday? And then only for a minute or two. Yet Tony has remembered it all.

The screen became brighter. 'What's that?' said Tony, interested.

'The enemy. The sun,' Brylo replied.

'What's the threat from the sun?'

'Communications, nothing else. But I don't like it, you can't predict it. They said that communication conditions aren't all that good – you must have heard those bursts of noise . . .'

'That's the sun?'

'Yes, and it's unpredictable. Good one minute, bad the next.'

'But you've already changed course, we're already heading away from the sun,' said Tony.

'It doesn't make much difference. Look, imagine that we're a grain of birdseed on the carpet of a big living-room. At the moment, we're somewhere in the middle of the room and it's taken us quite a time to get there. Meanwhile, there's a canary at the other end of the room and the cage door is open.'

'For flip's sake, why don't you just say what you mean?' began Tony. Brylo took no notice.

'The canary might notice us and it might not; we decide to retreat and get out of the way. We turn, and move away. Perhaps we move a whole six inches, even a foot. But what difference does that make to the canary?'

'The canary being the sun,' said Tony. 'Well, just for your information, the sun doesn't hop about like a canary.'

'No, but the stuff it sends out – the things that disturb our radio contact – they do hop about. Or so it seems. And you can't predict how far they jump.'

'I thought you scientific blokes had it all organized. Even

the sun. I thought you knew it all, solar radiation, sunspots, the lot . . .'

Once again, Brylo was surprised by Tony's choice of words. Solar radiation. Sunspots. Tony was quick . . .

'Look, think of the single canary seed on the carpet again,' Brylo said. 'If you don't *mind*, that is. Canary at one end of the room, right? Earth at the other. And somewhere in the middle, the grain of seed. Can't you see that nobody *can* know anything about the carpet — that nobody has ever explored the carpet before?' he paused, then said : 'You're right, Tony. I never should have brought in the carpet. We're not just a seed on a carpet, we're a seed on the whole of Greater London, or something like that. We're *tiny* ! And we're exploring, for the very first time, *this* !'

He pointed at the radar screen and pushed the lever. The black yet luminous carpet of nothingness traversed the screen, its movement suggested only by the minute traces left by the TV scanner itself. Once again, they saw a slight brightening of the glow as they passed the direction in which the sun lay, millions upon millions of miles away. Then the bright blackness again.

They stared silently for a long time, until Brylo whispered, 'Nothing. That's what we're looking at. Nothing at all. *Absolutely nothing!* No wind, no air, no life, no death. Absolutely nothing at all . . .'

As he spoke, what looked like a spark flashed a line across the screen and was gone.

'Nothing?' said Tony, in a low voice. 'You're sure?'

'I told you,' said Brylo, speaking like a sleepwalker from his dream of infinite space. 'It's only the TV. Even the light of the screen. . . . Only the TV itself. Nothing.'

Again a sudden, darting spark ! — so fast, that Tony had to close his eyes to 'photograph' it on his mind. 'It went the same way as the others,' he said. 'Right to left across the screen.'

Brylo came out of his trance, and looked at Tony. The

radio loudspeaker still said 'Dit, dit da, dit da dit, da, dit dit dit dit . . .' again and again. Brylo's eyes wandered. The neatly shaded lamps cast demure, correctly positioned pools of light on the consoles and desks and chairs of Control. There were his papers and his ballpoints, the only untidy things in the room . . .

'It's funny,' said Brylo, 'how, when you're tired, everything seems to freeze in position. Do you know what I mean? Everything seems to stand still, absolutely still . . .'

Although neither was looking at the TV, both saw out of the corners of their eyes the shower of sparks that fleetingly lit the screen. Both heard the quick, light, finger-tapping drumming of something small touching the side of the ship, as if a cat had made a lightning dab with its claws.

They saw the pools of light from the lamps shift and swim ever so slightly; and a single sheet of Brylo's papers detach itself from the pile and float, back and forth, to the floor.

'Nothing out there?' said Tony. 'I'm not so flippin' sure!'

Chapter 26

They contacted Earth.

'This is Harry Baines,' said the familiar voice. Somehow, the mere sound of it made them feel better, but the four-second pauses were agony. They explained what had happened.

'What is the screen showing now? Anything? Over,' said Harry Baines.

'Nothing at the moment,' said Brylo. 'No sparks. Nothing. Over.'

'Where was your TV scanner pointing when you saw the sparks? Over.'

'I don't know – Oh, yes I do, we haven't moved it ... I will take a reading. Hold on ... seventy-three degrees to left of ship. Seventy-three degrees to left of ship. Over.'

'Seventy-three degrees to left of ship, understood. That accounts for the apparent movement across the screen ...' They heard another voice talking to Harry Baines. Then, 'Yes, it seems clear enough. What has happened is this. You have run into some cosmic dust – some tiny particles of matter, the litter of space. It's a matter of chance – quite literally, infinite chance. Over.'

'Why did they give a trace like sparks on the screen? Over.'

'Because the scanner is situated amidships at the bottom of the spacecraft, and when the rim of the ship hit the particles, they broke up, leaving a radiation trace. As if they had been burning. Because your scanner was pointing sideways, the particles appeared to move sideways. Really you must have hit them straight ahead. Is that clear? Over.'

'Yes, I understand. What action do we take? Over . . .'

'First, you have red button-lights all over the ship to warn you if the skin of the ship is damaged. There are four or five in Control, near the ceiling. Have they lit up? Over.'

'No. Over.'

Tony grabbed the handset.

'This is Captain Tony speaking. What happens if we run into more of these flippin' particles? What happens if we hit a big one? What do we *do*? Over !'

'You have a number of self-sealing bulkheads in the ship, dividing it into . . .'

A storm of noise swamped the voice from Earth. And suddenly the screen was streaming with sparks !

Brylo leaped for the lever and traversed the TV scanner to the straight-ahead position. Now the sparks were like continuously exploding rocket burst, coming from the top of the screen and flowing past in a fan of slightly curved lines. It was like driving along a brilliantly lit road at a crazy speed. Sometimes, the stream would be interrupted as if the lights had all been switched off simultaneously. Brylo watched in a sort of ecstatic horror, his left hand fixed to the lever like a claw.

'The lights !' screamed Tony. 'For God's sake, the red lights have gone on !' He danced in a sort of writhing agony of urgency, stabbing his finger at the tiny red lights high on the walls. They gleamed on, off, on, off, in a regular pattern.

'We're holed !' gasped Brylo.

The loudspeaker spat out its crazy stream of howls and sputters and sharp explosions. More of Brylo's papers slipped off the desk and fluttered lazily to the floor. The pools of lamplight jigged and shimmered.

'The screen's gone black, we're through . . .'

'Or the flippin' scanner's bust . . .'

'No, there's another spark, the TV's working . . .'

'The air ! I'll check the air meters !'

Tony grabbed Brylo as he ran for the door. 'No, wait a sec. You check the air so that we know what we're losing, right? I'll switch on the ship's lights and use the TV ...'

'You can't! We don't know how to work the lights, we've never used them ...'

'Flippin' hell, that's right. OK, I'll check each room in the ship and see if the kids are all right ...'

'Get someone sensible to stand by the radio in here, we must get back in touch with Earth ...'

'Billy Bason. Now listen, be back here quickly as you can. Mustn't lose touch. Get back here pronto. OK?'

'OK! OK!'

Brylo dashed out. The loudspeaker said, '... on the left of the PPI display, just to the left of ...' Tony hesitated, cursed as the voice dissolved once again into madness, and hurtled after him.

Chapter 27

From Ashley's room there came a scream so intense and horrible that it seemed to wrap itself round Tony's ribs and squeeze them so that he could not breathe or move or think.

His terror of the scream held him for perhaps two seconds. Then, with a huge effort, he forced himself to move. He made himself breathe in a shuddering gulp of air; made himself relax his mouth from the contorted grimace in which it was set; made his brain obey his will.

But the scream ! Still it went on and on ! Still it pierced his very skull ! It was horrible, indecent, inhuman ... Suddenly Tony realized that it must truly be inhuman. And at the same instant he felt a strong draught around his ankles and noticed a chink of light under the door. The draught was blowing *into* there ...

He nerved himself, and flung open the door.

As he did so, he saw Ashley's folded handkerchief rise from a shelf, unfold itself in mid-air, fling itself across the room to the wall facing him, then disappear into the wall.

Tony yelled with terror and stepped backwards, blundering into a shelf. A notebook on the shelf rapidly turned the pages over one by one and stopped at a page with the words 'Dearest Mummy' written on it with a ballpoint. This page detached itself from the book, flew across the room in a straight line to the opposite wall, then disappeared into it. A sheet from the bed stood on end, climbed the wall and, bit by bit, fed itself into the wall until nothing was left.

The screaming stopped. Now there was a roar.

Tony swore ferociously, using every evil word he knew.

It did him good. Now he could feel himself trembling and despise himself. Now he could not only look, but see.

He saw that every loose object in the room was directed to the opposite wall. Jackplug cables on the Communications console idly raised themselves to a near-horizontal position, pointed to the opposite wall, then fell again. A dressing-gown cord lazily pointed itself, like an arm with a wagging finger, at the wall. Three pieces of paper scribbled with notes left Tony's pocket and, one after the other, crossed the room, entered the wall and disappeared into it.

Tony shuddered with fear and hate. '. . . you too !' he screamed. He picked up the earphones and flung them at the wall. They bounced off and fell on Ashley's bed.

Where was Ashley? His bed was a humped pile of sheets and blankets and pillows. Perhaps underneath that pile, Tony would find what remained of Ashley. . . . But he was past fear now. 'It's all a flippin' nightmare . . .' he muttered, and went over to the bed, the draught making his trousers flap like a ship's sail around his legs.

He fought the draught and tore at the bedclothes. He knew almost immediately that Ashley was not there and found himself shouting with laughter at the relief. As he bent over, he felt his hair pulling at his scalp. The draught was pulling it out straight towards the wall.

Suddenly, Brylo was beside him. 'You didn't go back to Control . . .' shouted Brylo above the roaring, but then stopped and stared at the wall. Where two panels should have joined in a neat, almost invisible line, there was a slit-like gap eighteen inches long and one inch wide. Brylo picked up a piece of notepaper from the pad and offered it to the slit. It was snatched from his fingers and disappeared.

'Ashley's not in beddy-byes !' yelled Tony, and began to laugh again, hysterically. Brylo tore at the wall panels and ripped off a whole section of wall. Beneath the panels, there were dully-gleaming alloy structural members and beyond them, a skin of metal. In the skin there was a small tear that nad rolled a strip of the metal skin into a neat spiral coil. A fragment of a sheet was gripped in the tear. The sheet was folded into incredibly tight creases, indicating the enormous suction pressure. Brylo pulled at a loose end of sheeting: instantly, the sheeting disappeared into the hole and the screaming started again.

Tony was doubled up. His eyes were filled with tears, his mouth was wide open and the laughter shook him so that the tears were jerked from his cheeks and sucked into the hole. Brylo slapped his face hard and he stopped laughing. Brylo fed a blanket into the hole. The screaming stopped and even the roaring quietened as more and more of the blanket squeezed itself into fold upon fold and locked into the mouth of the hole.

'I thought it was ghosts!' said Tony, feebly. He remembered the sheet. 'Ghosts wear sheets!' he said, and began laughing again. 'Ghosts! ... Sheets! ...' he choked. Brylo slapped him again and he stopped immediately. 'Cripes,' he said after some time. 'It was like a nightmare. You know, Brylo, when you wake up screaming ...'

'I believe you,' said Brylo. 'Ashley's with Tiddler and the others,' added Brylo. 'He's all right.'

Tony rubbed his face with his hands. 'What about the air? Vacuum outside, our air inside rushing out of the ship – that's what all this is about, right?' He pointed to the hole.

'Yes, that's it. Our air escaping. We've lost about a fifth of all we've got. That still leaves us ... enough,' said Brylo.

'How do you know?'

'Well, I'm assuming that we won't be up here for more than a couple of weeks. We ought to have plenty. Unless that hole can't be filled. Listen to it roaring ...'

Tony jumped up. He was very pale. 'Suppose it's not the only hole?'

'It is,' said Brylo. 'I've been right round. I didn't hear anything like this one anywhere else.' He kept to himself the thought that there might be further damage to the ship ...

damage that would reveal itself later on. And he refused to think of any further encounters with cosmic dust, let alone bigger fragments.

'And all the kids are all right?'

'Yes, Tony, they're fine. Really. I think you'd better get some sleep. You must have had it pretty bad in here.'

'It was flippin' horrible,' admitted Tony. 'Think I'll turn in for a couple of hours. You'll be back in Control?'

'Yes. All the warning lights have gone out, so we're not leaking badly any more.'

'Even then, I'd get someone to sleep outside this door, Brylo. You can't trust lights . . .'

Tony went. Brylo looked long and earnestly at the hole. There was still a huge surplus of blanket left on the inside. He tied it into a knot. If more of the blanket gets sucked through, he thought, the hole will still have to swallow the knot. And instead of swallowing it, it will tighten it.

Finally, he packed bits of blanket into every aperture he could find around the edges of the hole, until the roar was almost inaudible. Then he picked up the mattress, and laid it against the wall so that it covered the hole.

'So this is what it's like in the Space Age,' he murmured to himself wryly. Then he headed for Control.

Chapter 28

Communications were noisy but usable.

'Brylo, we're going to have to speed everything up,' said Harry Baines. Brylo thought that he knew Harry Baines well enough by now to detect a sharp edge of anxiety in his voice. 'And that means that you have got to work even harder, Brylo. I'll tell you the syllabus. Write it down. Acknowledge and over.'

'OK, am ready. But first tell me what you are worried about. I might as well know. Over.'

The pause, Brylo noticed, was still much the same duration. At least they were no further from Earth . . .

'We are anxious – not worried, Brylo – about the condition of the ship. There could be other damage to the skin. You might run into more particles, even, but that is not very likely. You can work out the odds for yourself – so many hours before you did actually hit something related to the number of hours it takes you to get back to Earth. And communications. They are not getting better, Brylo. From what we hear, we may be in for a spot of bother from the sun. Anyhow, we've decided to get you back here as fast as we possibly can. Which means that you've got an enormous amount of learning to do. Are you getting all this loud and clear? Over.'

'Loud and clear. Over.'

'All right. The first thing we will tackle is the "space drive". The nuclear motors. Now, these are strictly Model T – you know, Brylo, like a very early car engine. In other words, they are perfectly all right as long as you know all the tricks. The Flight Lieutenant didn't and that is why he died. Now, Brylo, I do not intend to tell you how the motors work because it doesn't matter to you. But I am going to take you a stage further in operating them.

'And particularly, I am going to explain to you how to use the displays on the consoles in front of you . . .'

It took hours. Then hours again as Harry Baines went over it all once more. When 'Over and out' was finally said, Brylo was too exhausted to notice more than two things: first, that he had drunk four cups of cocoa and eaten two plates of food; and second, that it was Tony who had brought him the food and drink – and that Tony had been there all the time and was still beside him now, his hands filled with pages of laborious, ill-written notes and his face set in a peculiarly determined expression that made Brylo uneasy.

An hour later Brylo was instructed by Earth to cut in the atomic motors. He did what he had been taught without any difficulties whatsoever and with surprisingly little difference to the sound and feel of the ship. Everyone was conscious now of a constant but distant sound of thunder. It was the motors. But not a tremor disturbed the ship. Nor had there been any feeling of acceleration. The motors, as Tony correctly explained to the others later, were brought in at quite high power – they were not 'slipped in' like starting a car from rest – but their power output was meaningless until translated into thrust. The power of the motors had to be given something to push against. This something was the ship itself. To begin with, the motors vented their power into space, where it had no effect. Later, and very gradually, 'vents' in the ship were closed: now, the motors' thrust pushed against the ship in one direction, and escaped through a sort of exhaust in the other.

'But . . . what's it all *look* like?' said Spadger. Tony turned to Brylo for an answer and Brylo turned to Tony. Neither knew. They laughed at the absurdity of it. 'Haven't the faintest flippin' idea!' said Tony.

'How fast are we going, then?' said Spadger.

'It isn't a matter of miles per hour at all,' said Brylo. 'Even if I could work it out – it wouldn't help us in any way. So I haven't the faintest flippin' idea !'

Everyone laughed.

Later that night, the time lag on the radio was down to three and a half seconds. They were heading for Earth and moving there fast.

'The rocket motors are something else again,' said Harry Baines. 'The atomic motors are your long-range, cruising motors so to speak. They take you from where you are now to within striking distance of making your landing on the moon . . .'

So it is the moon, thought Brylo. Oh, well . . .

'The rocket motors, on the other hand,' continued Harry Baines, 'are only used on two occasions : on take-off and landing. You've heard the term "Blast-off"? Well, the rocket motors do just that. They blast you off. Violently. You know what it's like, you experienced it when you left Little Mowlesbury . . .'

In fact, Brylo did not know. He had been made unconscious from the appalling acceleration. He shuddered at the memory, and let the point pass.

'Landing is just the same, but in reverse. You approach the moon, still under atomic drive, at an enormous speed – thousands of miles an hour. Hitting the atmosphere around the moon slows you down quite considerably – but you will still be going at an enormous rate. You therefore use the blast from the rockets as decelerators. You fire the rockets, the ship slows. You literally hold yourself off the surface you want to land on with rocket thrust. Are you hearing this loud and clear? Over.'

'Loud and clear. Why must we make the landing at all? Why can't we be transferred to another space craft, actually in space? Over.'

'Because you can't. Even if we could be sure of making the rendezvous successfully, there's no way of getting all of you from one ship to the other. Forget it. Right, we hold off with the rocket thrust. This is a very delicately balanced business – it was a miracle that the Flight Lieutenant ever made a landing at all ... in fact, he was able to land only because the whole business is more or less computerized. You do not have to decide the next stage, either, when you are very much closer to the surface you wish to land on – although you can override the computers if you think that your approach is going wrong. To make this clearer: the first stage is when you are approaching the moon, and if you looked out of a porthole you would have a view of part of the moon; the second stage, the nearest stage is when you are so close to the place where you want to land that if you looked out of the porthole, you could see most of an area the size of, say, Sussex. Is that clear? Over.'

'Loud and clear and understood. Over.'

'The final stage, like the other two, is computerized and automatic – BUT there is and must be a very considerable degree of human judgement. Your judgement, Brylo. At this final stage the village you came from – Little Mowlesbury – would be recognizable to you. You would be able to pick out the cricket pitch. Later, you would see people on it. Eventually, you would land on it. Whether you ploughed into it with an almighty thump or flopped on to it like a ton of bricks would depend on your ability to use the rockets to hold the craft off it for just the right length of time. The computers help, but you do it. Over.'

'Loud and clear and understood. Over.'

'Little Mowlesbury ...' said Tony, during the three-second pause that followed. 'The old cricket pitch, eh?' And once again, Brylo noticed the mask-like expression of determination that had frightened him before. He had little time to brood on it. Once the generalizations were over, his lessons on rocket drives, instrumentation and control techniques began. They lasted for four hours. At the end of them, he thought of nothing but sleep.

Chapter 29

The next day, communications got worse.

'Billy, have you seen anything on the TV screen? Any sparks or fireworks?' Tony asked.

'Not a thing,' said Billy, rather guiltily. He, Spadger and the Tiddler had been forced to give up their private world and to stand eight-hour watches in front of the TV screen. They disliked the new regime. But if there were to be further encounters with cosmic dust and debris, Tony intended to know about it in good time.

' "Not a thing, *Captain Tony*",' said Tony, eyeing Billy.

'Oh, all right – Captain Tony.'

'Brylo, what's the time lag?' asked Tony.

'Just under two seconds. We're more than half-way home – in terms of distance and time, anyhow.'

'What do you mean?'

'Well, the last bit is the tricky bit ... You know, the landing.'

'Nothing to it, Brylo boy!'

'Well, you haven't got to do it, have you?' Brylo replied.

'Ah yes, that's right. I haven't got to do it, have I?'

He left Control, whistling. He seems very cheerful, thought Brylo. And apart from his idiocy about making people call him 'Captain' (not that he ever tries that one on me), he is doing a wonderful job. Everyone has something to do, they all seem quite happy ...

At that moment, Sandra came in with his lunch. 'We've struck gold, Brylo!' she said grinning. 'We ran out of all those prepared dishes on plates and now we're on to the stuff I found in the deep freeze. Look!'

She put down the tray on Brylo's desk.

'Steak!' said Beauty. 'Oh, yummy, yummy!' She began to prance round Control. The gold and glitter of her was almost dazzling to Brylo, after his hours of dictation and learning and trial runs on the consoles. She seemed to beam light at him. Brylo beamed back at her.

'You didn't mind me bringing her?' said Sandra. 'She's being so good. She follows me everywhere, helping. That's what she calls it, helping. Fat help!' she ended loudly and managed to land a smack on Beauty's behind as she pranced by.

Beauty squeaked delightedly and began to call: 'You can't catch me! You can't catch me!'

Tony came in. 'What the flippin' heck . . .' he began, quite jovially. And he reached out his arms to catch Beauty. She stopped short and shrank back.

'Come on, Beauty!' said Tony, 'I'll catch you!'

Beauty went behind Sandra and clutched her legs. To Tony, she said, 'I don't like you. You hit me. And you haven't got nice white teeth like Brylo, yours are yellow.'

'Oh, they aren't yellow!' said Sandra, straining to keep her voice cheerful and easy. 'It's just that Brylo is so brown – Oh! . . .'

The five of them stood there. Brylo looked at Tony. He was white with rage. Everyone, he noticed, was looking at Tony.

'Yellow teeth, have I?' said Tony. 'Well, that's better than being a flippin' blackamoor, isn't it, Brylo?'

'I've been in the sun,' said Brylo and forced a laugh. It was a failure.

'Get her out of here,' said Tony, in a dead voice, pointing at Beauty.

Sandra and Beauty left. Billy stared hard at the TV screen, which showed nothing. And Brylo stared at his notes without seeing them. The whole thing is ridiculous, he thought –

but important. Very important. And yet he still could think of no reason why it should be. After all, what could *Tony* do?

'I'll show them . . .' muttered Tony, very quietly.

Chapter 30

Sometimes, the training sessions would go on so long that Brylo thought his head would split, and whatever fell out would lie pulsing on the table beside him. Brylo's Brains: pulse, pulse, pulse. He forced himself to smile at the thought, then wondered why he had bothered. It was not a particularly amusing thought. But then, he had always been a bit apologetic. The very opposite of Tony . . .

He looked at Tony. As usual, Tony sat a few feet from him, overhearing – no, listening to – every word. As usual, his notes were strewn around him. He was still writing. His large knobbly, efficient fist covered a lot of paper, creating a chaos of words. Yet again, Brylo asked himself, why does he bother? Why does he want to learn how the ship works? How can it benefit him?

Tony, aware that he was being stared at, suddenly looked up. His eyes and Brylo's locked in embarrassed surprise. They had hardly spoken to each other since the last quarrel. 'I won't be the first to drop my eyes,' thought Brylo.

Tony, still staring, said, 'You wonder why, don't you, Brylo boy?' and laughed. His eyes glittered with malice and amusement. Brylo could think of nothing to say in reply.

'I wonder why myself,' said Tony. He dropped his eyes and Brylo knew that he was lying, or about to lie. But why?

'I want to be the bright boy at school, that's what it is,' Tony continued. 'Bright like Brainy Brylo. There is Brylo the Brains, and there's Tony the Terrible Turk. That's it, isn't it Brylo boy?' He laughed.

'I've heard it all before,' said Brylo, flatly. 'Why don't you just shut up?'

Tea time for Teddy Bears,' said Tony, in a completely different voice. 'Time to listen with mother. Eight o'clock, get it?'

He nodded at the clock on the wall. There were footsteps outside, then all the children crowded into Control. At eight in the morning and at eight in the evening, the children spoke to their parents at home, on Earth. Brylo found it difficult to find words. So did Billy Bason and Spadger. The rest, though, just rattled on, talking about the food they had just eaten, or not forgetting to feed the rabbits and has the tortoise come home yet?

Di, however, spoke as if she were appearing in a very up-to-date documentary play about Parents and Teenagers and the gap separating them. She made her voice sound as if it were perpetually shrugging its shoulders. 'Are you *really* all right, Di darling?' said her mother with more than a hint of tears in her voice.

'Yeah, I'm all right, why shouldn't I be?' Di answered, shrugging off the question.

'We pray for you every night, your dad and me ...' said the voice, the tears very close.

'That's nice,' said Di, deliberately leaving a vacuum at the end of her words. And so it went on.

Tony either refused to speak to his parents at all, or used the talk as a way of advertising himself to the world.

'Are you all right, Tony?' said his mother (all the mothers began with that question).

'Everything's well under control on the ship,' replied Tony, 'I've got nothing to report that need cause any anxiety ...'

'But are *you* all right, you yourself, Tony?' said his father.

'Well,' answered Tony. 'The ship takes a lot of running. But we're all in good spirits and looking forward to a safe return.' He looked around the other children in Control as if expecting them to murmur agreement. Some of them actually did. 'Love to all of you from all of us,' he said finally; and Brylo was interested to see his cheeks flush slightly. He knew that was the wrong note to strike, thought Brylo. It was too slick. It sounded too like a commercial . . .

They left Ashley until last because they did not like to watch him and could not bear the sound of his mother's voice. As it mounted towards tears, then hysteria, they silently left Control without looking back at the stricken figure of Ashley, hypnotized by his mother's moanings and sobbings and endearments and beseechings. Generally, she was cut off when the time ran out at the very peak of her hysteria.

'It must be flippin' lovely in the studio, dealing with her,' said Tony. 'You know what? We're safer out here!'

Eventually, Sandra would go and get Ashley and lead him, tear-stained and shaking, back to his nest among the consoles in Communications. She hated this beyond all the many jobs she did.

'You're tired out, aren't you, Brylo?' said the voice of Harry Baines from Earth. 'Well, you've had a pretty gruelling time of it over the last day or so. But do you realize that you're nearly there? It's a fantastic operation they've got going on the Moon Station in your honour. . . . Look, I'll tell you what, you get yourself something to eat and drink and then sit back in a comfortable chair and listen to some of the tapes I've got. It's all stuff that you ought to know about, but on the other hand you don't have to understand it and work it yourself. Not like the extrapolaters, eh, Brylo?'

No, not like the extrapolaters, thought Brylo. Not like them, thank goodness. They had been an endless solid grind, repetition after repetition, dummy run after dummy run . . . He asked Sandra to send him in some food and drink, and settled down in the biggest chair.

'All right, here we are again,' said Harry keeping his voice bright and breezy. 'Now, I promised you these tapes about Moon Station and I think you'll find them fascinating, Brylo, fascinating! For instance, I've a few feet of tape here – not too much, Brylo, just the guts of the thing – from the men who started the Station. Karmesin, Strauss, Professors Desbrosses and Lutter from France and Germany ... and our own Professor Highan, of course, and the Japanese professor who helped so much with the environmental side. None of us could pronounce his name but it sounded something like "Eyespecs". So we called him that. Are you receiving? Over.'

'It's all right, Harry, you don't have to dress it up for me,' Brylo replied. 'Let's get on with it. I'll bet you are as tired as I am. Over.'

'All right, Brylo,' said Harry Baines, in his usual pleasant but decisive voice. 'As you say – let's get on with it. Now, about the conditions you may expect approaching the moon. You'll be able to use your TV of course, and you'll have no trouble at all with visibility. No fogs or clouds or anything like that. The gravitational pull of the moon is nothing like so strong as Earth's, so you will select the computer settings we have already discussed. We needn't do all that again, thank heaven. We'll skip all the procedures for landing the ship – you must know them better than I do by now – and talk instead of the conditions you will meet on landing. First, the surface. It really is ideal, Brylo. Very few areas on Earth offer anything to approach it, for two reasons. First, it doesn't matter if you miss by a hundred miles or so – no cities, no worries about hitting anything ...'

So I was right, thought Brylo. They are afraid of what might happen if we made a duff landing on Earth.

'... in fact, you can't very well miss the target area we have selected, it is several hundred miles wide in one direction. And it will be a soft landing. Better even than water ...'

Brylo's attention wandered. He looked across to where Tony sat. But Tony was not there!

Brylo interrupted Earth with the Call button and said, 'I'm sorry, Harry, I'm going over and out for ten minutes. There is something that I want to attend to here. Over.'

He switched off, got up and stared at Tony's vacant chair.

This was the first time, the very first time, that Tony had ever failed to listen to every word of Harry Baines' instruction. He had to find out why.

He found Tony in the 'VIP lounge'. Tony was sitting in a big leather armchair with a bottle of wine perched on one of its arms. Di sat on the other arm with a wineglass in her hand. When she saw Brylo, she gave Tony a drink from her glass and giggled. Tony felt embarrassed.

'Don't say old Brylo the Brain is going on the vino!' said Tony.

'Here, have some out of my glass!' said Di. She flapped her eyelashes at Brylo with mock sauciness and offered him the glass.

'Watch it, Brylo! She's after you!' Tony yelled. He was not drunk. Brylo could see the solid, unflinching malice in his eyes as he clowned.

Brylo took no notice of the glass and said, 'You weren't there.'

'Where, Brylo boy?'

'In Control.'

'He missed you!' squawked Di, hooting with laughter. 'He's a case!'

'Why should I be in Control, Brylo boy?' said Tony. 'Control with a capital C, that is. I'm in control anyhow. Get it?'

'He's a wizard with words,' said Di, nuzzling Tony.

'You weren't there. I thought something might have happened to you,' said Brylo. He was beginning to feel foolish.

'Oo, that would have been a worry, wouldn't it?' said Di. 'Tony die, Brylo cry. Inky, pinky, ponky!'

'Something come up, then?' said Tony innocently. 'Something the Captain ought to know about? We haven't run into a tram, or something, have we?'

'I didn't feel a shock,' said Di. 'But that's because I'm a shocker! Aren't I a shocker, Tony? Aren't I?' She poured herself more wine and spilt a dark patch on the leather.

'No, seriously Brylo boy,' said Tony, taking no notice of Di. 'What were they on about? Was it the moon? Was it about landing on the moon?'

'Yes,' began Brylo – then realized that Tony was playing with him. For how could Tony have known?

'Good place to land, the moon,' said Tony. 'Old Harry Baines said so. The great git.'

'How did you know?' said Brylo, trying to keep his voice steady.

'Miracle of electronics,' said Tony. 'Bet you couldn't say that, Di. Go on, try : Miracle of electronics !'

'Mirrick – mickle of . . .'

'*What* miracle of electronics?' said Brylo through his teeth.

'Oh, this,' said Tony. He lifted up a transistor radio, hidden by the arm of the chair. 'Good radio, this. Best transistor I've ever seen. Must be a new model. Gets Earth just like that, even on the frequency you and Harry Baines use. Of course, it works only one way, I can hear either you or Harry. I prefer old Harry. Talks a lot of sense, old Harry. Except when he goes on about the moon . . .'

Brylo put a hand up to his head, saw that the gesture had been noticed, and wished that he had not made it. What *was* it all about?

'I'm sorry, Tony, I don't get it. So you've found a nice little transistor radio and you know what Harry Baines was saying. All right, now what?'

'I didn't hear what old Harry was saying,' said Tony. 'Only the first bit. Then I switched off.'

'All right, you didn't hear. So *what*?'

'Flippin' moon . . .' said Tony. 'Raving on about the flippin' moon . . .'

'Who wants to go to the moon?' giggled Di.

'Look – stop messing about. You're not drunk, Tony . . .' began Brylo.

'Not so thunk as you drink I am !' said Di.

'What's all this about, Tony?' said Brylo, trying to sound calm but succeeding only in sounding desperate. 'What's so marvellous about the radio?'

Tony leaped to his feet and poked his head close to Brylo's. Then he yelled: 'IT WILL MAKE THE KIDS LAUGH!'

He's gone mad, Brylo thought. He even looks mad!

'Make 'em roar!' hooted Tony. 'There's old Brylo the Brains locked up in Control, working away at the radio, right? OK. Then there's old Brylo making a fool of me – me! – because he got the radio going and I didn't. Oh yes, I admit it – I must have looked a right Charlie after that meeting . . . but you wait till I just pull out the old transistor and get them the Light Programme! Who'll look a Charlie then?'

'You mean, all this is in aid of making the kids laugh? Simply so that you can say "Look, I'm cleverer than Brylo, I can get Earth on a transistor"?' asked Brylo, astonished. Tony did not answer. He walked up and down, poured himself another glassful of wine and drank it at a gulp.

'Look, Tony, I don't like you either. If you want to make a fool of yourself by playing charades with transistor sets, do it and be happy. All I care about is getting this ship to the moon . . .'

'He's doing it again, Di!' said Tony. 'The moon! Old Brylo and the moon! What's all this chat about the moon, Brylo boy? What makes you think that we'll end up on the moon?'

'Because that's where the Moon Station is and that's where the landing is going to be!' shouted Brylo. 'Surely your precious transistor made you understand that?'

'Moony, Loony,' said Di, winking at Tony. Brylo felt lost.

Then Spadger rushed in. 'They're calling you, Brylo!' he shouted. 'They want you on the radio! Come to Control, quick!'

Brylo and Tony ran to Control to encounter a double disaster and the beginnings of a third.

The TV screen spattered with spark-like traces, telling them that they had run into another patch of cosmic debris: and the voice of Harry Baines over the loudspeaker was barely audible over the mad racket of interference. They could just distinguish the repeated words.

'Come in, Brylo! Come in, Brylo! Over!'

Brylo flicked the switch and began sending to Earth. 'Harry, this is Brylo. Harry, this is Brylo. Are you receiving? Over.'

After a pause – less than two seconds now – the voice from Earth replied. 'I heard you, Brylo. Just. I will test, starting now. One, two . . . five . . . seven, eight, nine . . .' The other numbers were blotted out by the shrieks and howls and gun-shot noises of the interference. Brylo raised an eyebrow at Tony, flicked the switch, and replied to Harry: 'Harry, this is Brylo. Brylo speaking. Your test gave me "one, five, seven, eight, nine". That is bad. Reception is bad. I will test, starting now . . .' Like Harry, he spoke the numbers one to ten and awaited Harry's check-back.

'This is Harry, Brylo . . . Harry speaking. I received only "four, five, six" and "over". Doesn't look too good, Brylo . . .' Brylo and Tony picked up a few words and sentences that made some sense: 'sunspot activity . . . Mount Palomar reports solar . . . worried about damage to the ship . . .'

Brylo replied briefly and asked for instructions. The strain of listening through the noise to Harry's voice hurt his head.

Harry said, 'We're bringing you in, Brylo. Bringing you into Moon Station as quickly as we can. No more lessons, repeat no more lessons and instructions. We must get you out of the belt of debris . . .'

Brylo glanced at the TV screen. The trails of sparks were frightening. He noticed that Tony's eyes were shifting from the sparks to the red lights, still unlit, and back again.

Harry began to shout a series of instructions, repeating each three times. Brylo had no time to be frightened of their meaning. He merely obeyed them. A quarter of an hour later, Harry went off the air for a few minutes to consult with his advisers. Brylo thankfully cut off the radio entirely.

But the usual silence did not greet him. Instead, the sound of thunder filled the Control cabin. 'Look . . .' said Tony, pointing at the desk lamps. The pools of light they cast were shimmering and shivering.

'We're going at a fair old lick?' he asked.

Brylo checked the dials in front of him. 'We're going pretty well flat out on the space drive – the nuclear reaction drive. And we've turned. We're going like – like I don't know what. I suppose it must be as fast as anyone has ever travelled . . .'

'That's why we're vibrating?'

'I suppose so. Just listen to the noise . . . And, of course, we're not travelling in a straight line – although I don't know if that makes any difference. We've changed course.'

'Changed course!' said Tony. 'You mean we're not heading for the moon?'

'Oh, yes, we're heading for the moon all right – but they've put us on an arc, a curve. I suppose they want to get us out of the debris belt.'

'But they're still heading us for the moon?' said Tony, thoughtfully. He muttered something that Brylo did not catch, then looked hard at the TV screen. The sparks were still intermittently filling it, and Tony made a face. 'Try the radio again, just for a second.' Tony switched on. The noise was as bad as ever.

126

'I don't think they're connected – the debris and the noise,' said Brylo. He found it difficult to keep his eyes off the dull red dots of the warning lamps. He expected, every moment, that they would light. And then –

Earth flashed them. Brylo switched on the radio and the thunder of the reaction drive was once again flooded out by the din from the loudspeaker. They heard little of what Harry said, but what they did pick up made them exchange glances.

'Eight hours!' whistled Tony. 'In eight hours, he said! We'll be hitting the moon in eight hours!'

'Not hitting it,' said Brylo, with an uneasy laugh. Tony thought, then said: 'Dead right, Brylo boy! That's one thing we won't be doing!'

Before Brylo had time to try and work out what Tony could have meant, Harry was on the radio again and Tony had left the room.

Chapter 32

Tony held a meeting in his cabin. Everyone attended. He told them, clearly and without his usual dramatics, that they might be landing within twelve hours. He explained the difficulties they were having with communications and cosmic dust. He told them what they were to do as soon as the landing signal, a siren that sounded in every part of the ship, was sounded: they were to come to his cabin, sit in the chairs, and use the straps fitted within the chairs to secure themselves.

'We'll try it now,' he said. 'Each of you go to a leather chair. No, it doesn't matter which one, Spadger. But when you've chosen your chair, remember it and go back to it when the time comes for landing. Right you've all got chairs? OK, put your hands in the holes in the arms and you'll feel the straps and buckles. No, don't fiddle about – let's start again, watch me!'

He showed them how to wear and fix the straps, which were very like a full harness car safety-belt. Brylo noticed that he remembered every detail of the straps – which part of the harness went on first, how the locks operated, just how tightly the straps should be secured. I wonder if he's been practising? he thought, then decided against it, and realized yet again what a good brain and memory Tony had.

'All right, the release.' Tony hit the buckle and the harness fell apart. 'Now, we'll all do it. Sandra, you can do Beauty's when the time comes, and Billy, you can make sure Ashley's all right. Brylo, you and me will be in Control, but we might as well get all the practice we can, so let's go through it.'

He's even being tactful, thought Brylo. Not making Ashley look small. Not trying to make me look a fool ...

'No, Sandra, do your own strap this time. I'll attend to Beauty.' Tony moved over to Beauty who looked at him uncertainly. But Tony gently went through the business of strapping her into her seat and said, 'OK?' when he had finished. She nodded, reassured. 'All right, let's see you get out,' said Tony. Beauty hesitated. 'You remember,' said Tony, 'all you do is give it a bang! Go on, you can do it!'

'Go bang!' said Beauty, hitting the buckle with her little fist. She laughed delightedly into Tony's face as the straps fell away and smiled after him as he ruffled her hair and moved on to help Ashley.

Friends again, thought Brylo; then felt mean for having had the thought.

'All right, do it as often as you like, you might as well get used to it,' said Tony, returning to his chair. 'But listen to me while you practise. First, about eating. No one is to eat or drink after tea. Billy, you lock up the kitchen. You can't land on a full stomach. Right?' They nodded.

'Second, stay in your own cabins whenever possible until the siren goes. I want everyone to be in their usual places so that I – or Di, or Billy – know where to find you. When you hear the siren, come to this cabin and go to the chairs you sit in now.'

He stood up. 'Third,' he said impressively. 'I don't want anyone in Control. Nobody. Nobody at all! Nobody, that is but me, and Brylo and Di ...'

'Di?' said Brylo, shocked.

'Yes, Di,' said Tony, pretending to be surprised at Brylo's tone. 'She's our go-between. We've got to have someone connecting us in Control with the others outside, haven't we? Well, *haven't* we?'

Brylo muttered, 'I suppose so.' Too late he remembered that there was a loudspeaker link from Control to all the cabins. Why did Tony want Di in Control?

But by now, the meeting was over and the children were dispersing.

'It's fantastic!' whispered Brylo. 'It's the most fantastic thing I've ever seen!'

'It's the most fantastic thing anyone's ever seen,' said Tony, hoarsely. 'I mean, for flip's sake . . . just look at it!'

It was the moon. It filled the TV screen, then spilled over its edges as Tony lengthened the focus of the lens. He turned the knob to its utmost, but the picture lost sharpness. 'I suppose it's a freak picture, we're lucky to get it this far out . . .'

'Bring it back again,' said Brylo, still whispering, and gazed at the reformed picture with awe and wonder.

'Can't see the Man on the Moon!' said Di pertly, jarring him out of his mood. Brylo wondered whether it was worthwhile suggesting that they could do without Di, and decided not to. Too late again . . .

Harry Baines' voice came through. The reception was still apalling. 'Within an hour, Brylo, you'll be resetting the computers for the Approach phase and adding manual corrections,' he said. It seemed unreal to Brylo. Everything seemed unreal to him since he had seen the moon.

'Start Approach procedure!' said Harry Baines. His voice was almost metallic now, as hard and precise as a machine. He began to dictate a series of co-ordinates. Brylo fed them into the instruments in front of them.

'Down to 38,000. Three Eight. Over,' said Harry.

'Three eight. Three eight. Over.' The thunder that had shaken the ship for so many hours softened a little: the pools of light from the lamps steadied.

'You're showing a drift from No. 3 computer. Over.'

'OK, am correcting drift, will read the first threes as I correct. Two four one, seven three one, nine four five. Hold for five seconds . . .'

Brylo glanced at Tony and was astonished by the fixity, the complete concentration, of his face. Tony's lips moved as he repeated the figures Brylo had just read: Brylo could see that he was reading them, correctly, from the crossed pointers. Suddenly Tony felt or saw that Brylo was watching him. Immediately, he switched on a loose grin and wagged his head. 'Too brainy for me, Brylo boy,' he said, clownishly. Brylo knew very well that he was lying.

'All right, Brylo,' said Harry's voice. 'Your set of first threes will do for five minutes. No drift now, you are on corrected computer course. Keep those readings for five minutes. Over and out.'

'How close are we now, Brylo boy?' Tony asked.

'Another hour and we'll be thinking about the actual landing. Don't you want to go round the ship and warn the kids?'

Tony beckoned Di. 'Go and find out what the kids are doing and tell them to stop it,' he said jovially. 'Make sure they're all where they ought to be. Then get back here fast.'

Di returned three minutes later. 'They're all right,' she said. 'That stupid little perisher Ashley is sitting on his bed pretending to talk to Mummy, as per usual. He gives me the willies...'

Harry's voice came over the loudspeaker. 'Brylo, how about the touchdown drill? Anything you want to go over again? Over.'

'No, there's nothing ...' began Brylo. But Tony took the microphone from his hands.

'Captain Tony speaking, Harry. Look, why don't you give us a brief run through on the touchdown procedure? It can't do Brylo any harm to hear it again and – well, you know, in case anything happens ...'

Brylo took the microphone and said, 'There's really no need, Harry. Over.'

Yet Tony had his way. For seven minutes, Brylo half-listened while Harry went through the drills he knew so well. Tony listened avidly to every word. Again Brylo found himself asking, *why?*

And now, the TV screen showed the face of the moon so clear and so near that Brylo thought he could pick out the Moon Station itself.

'Those dots – that could be it!' he said, pointing to minute specks near the centre of the screen.

'Could be,' said Tony lazily, not bothering to look.

'But don't you see – we're looking at the very place we'll land! From now on, the screen shows only the exact area we're interested in. The nearer we get, the more detail we will see!'

'Stone *me*,' said Tony. Then he leaned over to Di and asked her to go and get them a hot drink.

He's not interested at all, thought Brylo. *Why?*

Ten minutes later, the screen showed so distinct a picture that you could pick out small, individual irregularities on the moon's surface.

'I suppose we're seeing an area about the size of a smallish town!' said Brylo, craning forward to peer at every detail.

'Looks a pretty dull old town,' commented Tony.

'Well, that's the whole point, don't you see? They want to land us on the most featureless place they can find. No hills, no valleys – everything flat.'

'Yeah, dead flat,' said Tony and actually yawned. 'Any more of this poison, Di?' he said, holding out his cup. 'I'm parched.'

A little while later, Brylo said, 'It's about time we alerted the kids – we ought to get them into your room and see they're ready for the landing . . .'

'No hurry, Brylo,' said Tony.

'But for heaven's sake, Tony!'

'Doesn't old Brylo get excited?' Tony asked Di.

'Yes, doing his nut just because we're going to the moon!' said Di, picking at one of her fingernails. 'Never fancied the place myself . . .'

The loudspeakers crackled and Harry Baines came in. 'Brylo, you're getting to the last stage. This is just about it. As soon as the computers say so, switch in rocket drive and then follow the drill. Follow the drill, Brylo! that's the thing that matters most. Don't get panicky. Don't do anything violently. Remember the enormous forces under your control. But above all, remember to follow the drill! Over.'

Brylo turned to Tony. 'Get them into their seats, Tony,' he said flatly. 'You've only got five minutes before I cut the rockets in. Please get started.'

Both he and Di rose to their feet and stood over him, Tony smiling and Di with an odd, set expression on her face.

'Sure thing, Brylo boy!' said Tony. 'I think we'll start with – *you!*'

Just before Di held him and Tony hit him, Brylo thought to himself, 'Now all my questions are answered. Now I know why!'

Then the blow fell and he was unconscious.

Chapter 33

When he came to, Tony was hard at work. He heard Brylo groan and then speak, but did not bother to turn round. 'See to him Di !' he said, casually.

Brylo found that he could hardly move. Tony and Di had lashed him to his chair not only with the safety harness but also with bits of webbing. This did not surprise him in the least.

'So we're not going to the moon, Tony?'

'No, Brylo boy. Di doesn't fancy it.'

'That's right,' said Di, mopping the bruise on Brylo's head with a cold cloth. His head and neck were very painful.

'You're heading for Earth?' said Brylo.

'Of course, Brylo boy. Good old Earth. You and your flippin' moon ! Who wants to land on the moon, for flip's sake?'

'I think you're barmy,' said Brylo, in a despair so complete that he did not bother to raise his voice.

'I'm surprised you didn't cotton on, Brylo boy,' said Tony, studying the instruments in front of him. 'But you're only brainy in certain ways, aren't you? You don't really know anything about anything, do you? And when you learn, you learn too late, don't you? Brainy Brylo – don't make me laugh !' He gave a false laugh, but still continued to survey the instruments.

'What about Harry ...'

'Oh, he's gone over and out until I'm ready for him,' said Tony. 'Switched off at the mains, so to speak. He didn't half carry on, didn't he, Di?'

'Alarming,' said Di, rinsing out the cloth in cold water.

134

'We told him you'd had a nervous breakdown,' she added, casually.

'How much longer until we get close to Earth – close enough to use the rockets?' said Brylo miserably.

'Seventy three minutes.'

'*Seventy-three minutes!*' Brylo jerked in his chair and his mind raced. 'But that's not possible!'

'You've had a nice long byebyes,' said Di, holding a small bottle in front of Brylo. 'Hours and hours. I found these in the medical room . . .'

'And if you don't shut up,' interrupted Tony, 'we'll give you a few more!'

There was silence for a minute. A light flashed on the console. 'That'll be Harry,' said Tony. 'He never seems to learn, does he? Still can't remember who's captain of the ship . . .' He flicked a switch and the light went out. 'No interruptions, please!' he said to the light. 'Captain's orders!'

'That's what it's all about, isn't it Tony? What a fool I was not to have known! Captain Tony. *Captain* Tony! You and Di – all you want is the big film-star reception! You can't get it on the moon, so we've got to go to Earth! There'll be the press cameras and the TV cameras and the film cameras – and then the door opens, and out comes Captain Tony, the boy wonder!'

'And what's wrong with that, you chocolate coloured git?' screamed Tony, swinging his chair round. 'Look, I've had enough of you, you . . . bright boys, you brainy kids! . . . Yes teacher, no teacher! . . . You make me *sick*! Because you don't know from *nothing*! Who done all the things that really matter on this trip? *Me!* Who just sat and did his lessons like a good little boy and expects to get all the credit? You! Well, you flippin' won't get it, because I earned it, I want it, I'll get it! I'll show them! I'll show them all . . .'

He spun the chair round violently to hide his distorted face. Di, keeping her face completely neutral, said, 'Well there you are, Brylo boy. Captain Tony wants to be It, and

I want him to be It and you're strapped up in a chair. Looks as if he's going to get his way, doesn't it?'

There was silence until Tony said, 'Well, it's time I called old Harry. Almost rocket time, Brylo boy, and even old Harry has his uses.'

He operated the controls of the TV. On the screen, Brylo saw Earth – a great curve that filled the screen, patched with light areas that could be clouds.

'But we're close! We're too close!' said Brylo, suddenly sick with fear.

'We can't be . . .' muttered Tony, frantically jerking his head at one dial then another.

'Get Harry!'

Tony's fingers lashed at switches. The loudspeaker hummed – then stayed humming. Tony started at it, his mouth open. 'We're not getting a signal!' he muttered.

'It's that little perisher Ashley!' screamed Di. They ran out of the room and Brylo could hear them in the distance pounding on the Communications door. Then Beauty came in.

Chapter 34

'It's being dull,' said Beauty. 'I can't find anybody! Why are you all tied up? Oh, I know. Tony said you were bad . . .'

'Get me *out*!' said Brylo.

Beauty stared at him uncertainly.

'Beauty, you've got to get me out of this chair! Help me undo these straps! You *must*, Beauty!'

'Tony said you were silly!' said Beauty. 'He made a joke, it was about a – a transistor, and everyone laughed.' Brylo heard the Communications door open, and a shrill wail from Ashley.

'I laughed,' said Beauty, as if in proof of what she was saying.

'Please, Beauty, please!' Brylo hissed. 'Undo these straps! These straps round my arms!'

Beauty did not move. What argument would make her act?

'They're hurting me!' said Brylo.

'Oh dear,' said Beauty. 'Which ones?'

'Please, Beauty! These ones! Undo these ones! The ones round my arms!'

Brylo watched the smooth, pretty, useless little hands pull and tug. At last a strap gave, then another loosened. 'It's hard,' said Beauty. And at that moment, the loudspeaker boomed out Harry's voice and Tony and Di ran back into the room.

'What the –!' shouted Tony, striding over to Beauty, his hand raised.

'Don't hit me!' said Beauty, with a tiny dignity that stopped Tony. 'You hit me before!' she said, then lost her courage and ran from the room.

Tony glared at the loudspeakers, at Brylo, at Di. 'Get after her! Find out what the kids are doing! For flip's sake ...'

He ran to his chair and listened to Harry: '... dangerously close, you have only minutes! Come in, Tony! Come in, Tony! Over!'

'It's me,' said Tony, his voice shrill. 'It's Tony speaking! Give me instructions! Over!'

'Thank God! We thought you'd ... Never mind, here are your instructions. Set these co-ordinates on the displays marked F, G and H. Are you ready? Over.'

'Ready! Over.'

The numbers poured from the loudspeaker, cold, clear and incessant. Tony worked fast to begin with, then began to lag. 'Steady on, steady on!' he shouted. But he had not switched the microphone on and no one heard him but Brylo.

Brylo watched, tugged at his bonds and tried to understand what Tony was doing or failing to do. Tony's missing some of them! he thought, he's not setting them, he's not relating them to the computer readings, he doesn't know the drill ... In an agony of impatience, he tore the flesh of his wrists on the straps. They did not yield.

Suddenly he noticed that Control was filling with the children.

'You're too late! Too late! Bring in the rocket drive, Tony, bring in the rockets! I'll give you the settings, are you ready, over!'

The children clustered in the centre of the room, gaping at the TV screen. Now, it was filled with an image of dark and light, cloud and land, that very slowly tilted and swung.

'Are you ready? Are you ready? Acknowledge and over!' shouted Harry's voice.

'I'm ready! Over!' said Tony. Again he forgot to operate the microphone switch, then remembered too late.

'... on your left to 320, three two oh, then synchronize

with the computer readings on the same console! Got that? Acknowledge and over!'

Tony was almost sobbing. 'He's going too flippin' fast, the stupid great git – too *fast* . . .'

The children were staring at him. Sandra drew Beauty close to her.

The picture on the screen showed the same steady swing of what could be cloud and could be land – a meaningless picture that nevertheless showed them the shadow of death. For now the picture seemed closer . . .

'Tony, for God's sake, let me take over!' Sandra moved to Brylo's side as he spoke, and stood ready to set him free, her face turned to Tony. Tony rose to his feet, his eyes glittering.

'Don't you touch him!' he screamed. 'Don't any of you touch him! I'll do the one that goes near him! I'll smash his head in! I'm the Captain! Can't you understand, *I'm the Captain!*'

His voice cracked into a screech. Not one of the children moved.

'Leave him alone,' said Di, huskily. 'He'll do what he says. He'll kill you.'

The scene was frozen in time. The lights inside Control made the alloy tube that Tony held glint in his hand. The loudspeaker hummed almost soothingly. Only the picture on the screen moved with a slow, uninterrupted, gentle swing. And each swing seemed to bring them nearer.

It was Beauty who broke the spell. She firmly removed Sandra's hand from her shoulder, and walked, very upright, to Brylo's side and began tugging at the straps. Tony made an inarticulate sound: she turned to face him and said, 'They hurt him,' and went on with her work.

Spadger silently joined her. Then Billy Bason, then the Tiddler, then the others. The straps were off. Only the harness remained. 'You have to bang it,' said Beauty, and tapped it with her plump, honey-coloured fist. The harness fell away.

There was a clatter as Tony let fall the alloy tube: then

complete silence as he slumped into another chair and Brylo took over.

'Give me the co-ordinates, Harry, Over.'

'Brylo? Thank heaven! Right, set these: three one eight and lock in your laterals. Interrupt me when you want to . . .'

'Laterals locked. Over.'

'Three one five and hold. Now integers only: five, five, four, four, four, three . . .'

'Give me a time elapse. Over.'

'Time elapse nine, but you've got that showing here anyhow. Fine! Three, three, two, two, two, two, one . . . Three-ten! Don't confirm, just follow the integers . . .'

The TV screen showed the face of Earth, steady now and advancing. By the light of the screens, the silent children watched Brylo's face. It too was steady. His brown hands moved almost lazily over the console; but with complete sureness.

'Is it going to be all right?' asked Beauty.

'Yes,' said Sandra. 'Quite all right. Now, shh . . .'

Chapter 35

In the evening sky, there appeared a golden dot – a disc that caught the evening sun. It grew in size and the world watched it grow. It made the sound of thunder, and the world listened and trembled. There was the roaring of a thousand express trains and the shattering blast of a thousand cannon: grass withered to grey ash instantly, and a tall oak that had grown for more than a century was made carbon and dust in seconds. The world clasped its hands in a frantic prayer: and the space ship hovered, dipped – and at last, landed.

For a time, the world forgot to talk of wars and strikes and politicians and scandals. For the heart and mind of the world had for once been left to itself and had reached out to the children, high above Earth, adrift in the endless enormity of Nothing. But now the world found its breath again and wagged its tongue and talked the usual nonsense.

'They're all barmy,' said Brylo to Sandra, a week after the landing. 'But it isn't until after a thing like this happens that you realize just how barmy.' He rolled over in the long grass and watched Spadger showing Billy Bason how Red Indians squat on their heels.

'They can keep it up for hours,' said Spadger.

In the middle of Little Mowlesbury's meadow, Tony swung his bat in a ferocious swipe. As usual, it connected – this time with such violence that he didn't bother to run. Instead he strolled over to Di and Brylo and flung himself down beside them. 'Got my twenty,' he announced, rather too casually. 'Did you read the papers today? Make you flippin' sick. *"The Angels of Space!"* Read that one, Di?'

'Dead right I'm angelic,' said Di, fluttering her eyelashes.

'I've got one here that's a giggle!' said Billy Bason, pulling a piece of newspaper out of his pocket. 'Listen to this: "*The heroine of space is six today!*" It's her birthday, Beauty's birthday, get it? Heroine of Space ...!'

Tony and Brylo exchanged glances. Tony said, very quietly, 'Come to think of it, Brylo boy, that's something near the flippin' truth.' It was an admission: and an offer of friendship.

There was a long pause. Then Brylo winked and said, 'Look at Big Chief Spadger giving himself Red Indian cramp! Go on, Tony, you're nearest!'

Tony stretched out a foot, delicately inserted it under Spadger's knee, and lifted.

Sure enough, Spadger fell over backwards.

Heard about the Puffin Club?

... it's a way of finding out more about Puffin books and authors, of winning prizes (in competitions), sharing jokes, a secret code, and perhaps seeing your name in print! When you join you get a copy of our magazine, *Puffin Post*, sent to you four times a year, a badge and a membership book.
For details of subscription and an application form, send a stamped addressed envelope to:

The Puffin Club Dept A
Penguin Books Limited
Bath Road
Harmondsworth
Middlesex UB7 ODA

and if you live in Australia, please write to:

The Australian Puffin Club
Penguin Books Australia Limited
P.O. Box 257
Ringwood
Victoria 3134